"*The Lion's Heart* moved me to the core. Dena Hunt managed a rare feat: a delicately crafted novel that is at once a work of beauty and existential weight, and yet forces you to keep reading with all the urgency of a thriller."

Bernardo Aparicio Garcia
Publisher, *Dappled Things*

"Dena Hunt is a consummate storyteller who does not shirk or shy away from the difficult questions about life and love that her story raises. *The Lion's Heart* contains not only the loves of lovers, spouses, parents and children, but also the demons and dragons that selfishness unleashes. *The Lion's Heart* is not for the faint-hearted, nor is it for the hard-hearted. It pulsates with a passion that will bring true hearts to their knees."

Joseph Pearce
author of "*The Unmasking of Oscar Wilde*,"
co-editor of the St. Austin Review

"Dena Hunt conveys some of the very real struggles of those persons who have same-sex attractions (SSA), especially the shame, confusion, and misery that can accompany such feelings. She shows how that suffering can affect family and friends. The path to understanding homosexuality requires abundant patience, prudence and good will because the topic is not primarily a controversial cultural issue, but rather a complex personal reality. It is one for which there is not one simple or general explanation— or response. This novel gives us a glimpse into the lives and hearts of those touched by SSA who are striving to understand themselves, and so to love genuinely after the example of Jesus Christ and the teachings of His Church."

Rev. Paul Check
Executive Director, Courage International

D1475131

The Lion's Heart

A Novel

Dena Hunt

FQ Publishing

Pakenham, Ontario

Copyright © 2014 Dena Hunt
The Lion's Heart, Second Edition
All rights reserved.
ISBN: 978-0-9879153-7-5
Editor: Ellen Gable Hrkach

Photo Credit/Copyright Attribution: Artur Bogacki/Shutterstock

Published by FQ Publishing
PO Box 244
Pakenham Ontario K0A2X0
Canada

www.fullquiverpublishing.com

National Library of Canada in Publication

Printed in the United States of America

The author is donating 100 percent of the royalties from this book to charitable organizations.

Dedication

*For Jay
and for all courageous
men and women*

PART I

APRIL

CHAPTER ONE

It was raining.

Why did it rain every time he had to pick up Roxanne from school? He turned the Lexus through the stone gateway of St. Joseph's Academy and followed the smooth, wet asphalt drive around the manicured lawn. He thus joined the line of cars waiting their turn to pull up to the covered portico, one car at a time. It took parents twice as long to pick up their children when it was raining.

Max was irritated, and irritated with himself for being irritated. He finally saw Roxanne at the edge of a cluster of bouncing, chattering girls, all in the blue and white plaid skirts of St. Joseph's uniforms, her long, blond braid hanging over the shoulder of her navy cardigan. She saw him, turned on a big smile, and waved wildly, as though she hadn't seen him in six months. His heart tightened. God, she was beautiful! All irritation vanished.

The rear door opened, her book bag was thrown across the back seat, and Roxanne leaned over the driver's seat to put both arms around his neck and kiss him with a loud smack on his cheek.

"Hi, Daddy!"

"Hello, girlfriend. Sit down and buckle up. There's a long line of cars waiting behind us."

She obeyed. Roxie was a good girl as well as beautiful—he and Michelle had been blessed. She was eleven years old now, and he had no news yet of puberty's arrival. Whether she'd be a good girl then remained to be seen. Jake, his fifteen-year-old son, was "good" at that age too. Now he was a cause of constant concern, if not constant worry. What was it about puberty that just destroyed kids? Max had a habit of asking himself questions he never answered.

"Daddy, are we going to the lake this weekend? Is Jake coming home? If we don't go to the lake, do you think we could go to Six Flags? We haven't been in ages!"

"Okay, which one of those questions do you want answered first?" He looked at her in the rear-view mirror.

She unwrapped a piece of gum and popped it into her mouth.

"Don't throw that gum wrapper out the window. Save it till you get home to put it in the trash can."

"Okay. Well, first, is Jake coming home?"

"No. He's staying with a friend in Highland."

"What? He hasn't been home in a month!"

She was genuinely disappointed. His children actually loved each other; he and Michelle were lucky there, too.

Siblings usually bickered—and worse—but Jake was very affectionate with his little sister, and Roxanne idolized him.

"Well, honey, he's got a chance to go hiking in the mountains up there with his friends. You don't want him to pass that up, do you?"

"Noooo," she answered slowly, chewing gum and looking out the rain-splashed window in a little pout.

He smiled at her in the mirror: "And yes—we're going to the lake."

"Yayyy!"

Allen Martin Maxwell, Jr., was indeed a lucky man. A junior partner of the law firm of Federer, Johnston, and Maxwell in Atlanta, specializing in trusts, wills, estate-planning and such, he had a dull but exceptionally lucrative job. His wife, Michelle, was a beautiful blonde, his sweetheart ever since they were teenagers, actually. They'd been married seventeen years, but he could not remember a time when she wasn't there. She was from South Carolina, but they'd gone to summer camp together as children. Everybody in the family was in good health, except for a few minor problems, like his rising blood-pressure. Michelle had a job she enjoyed at an art gallery. True, their son, Jacob, was caught with some of his buddies at school last year with marijuana, but he and Michelle decided to send him to a prep school in North Carolina that had a reputation for instilling character. And so far, so good. The most worrisome thing about Jake, really, Max thought, was that he was so secretive. Sometimes it seemed as though he'd left them somehow, and not just because he was going to school away from home.

He pressed the remote and the garage door went up. They pulled in the driveway and he saw Michelle's car already there. He wondered if she'd started packing for the houseboat they kept on Lake Lanier.

Roxanne slammed the car door and ran up the steps to the kitchen, dragging her book bag up the steps behind her.

He got out of the car. "Hey, little girl! I didn't ask you: Do you have homework this weekend?"

She ignored him. When they got inside, Michelle leaned over the kitchen island to accept her daughter's kiss.

"Didn't your daddy ask you about homework?" she asked.

"It's just a little bit. I have to read a chapter in history and do some math problems."

Max slipped off his tie and unfastened the top button of his shirt. "You can take your books with you to the lake. Just leave your bag right here by the door so you won't forget it."

He turned to Michelle. "Have you started to pack yet?"

"Good grief, Max. I just got here. Give me a break."

He noted that she'd been home long enough to pour a glass of wine, though. Sometimes he thought Michelle was drinking too much. She looked great in her blue silk shirt and linen pants, but he wondered if that little paunch she'd developed—so slight that only he would notice it—might not be the effect of a bit too much wine.

"Well, did you have a good day?" he asked.

Her brow puckered, as if she didn't know how to answer that simple question. "Hunter's has a new director."

"Yes, I know, but he's been there for a while, hasn't he?

You told me about him at least two months ago. Has he suddenly started giving you some kind of problem?"

"No, not really." She moved a falling strand of hair back behind her ear and took a meditative sip of her wine. "It's just—I don't know. Something about him bothers me."

Roxanne came running downstairs in her swimsuit and headed for the glass doors that led to the pool.

"Wait a minute, Roxie. Why don't you get your homework done now so you won't have to take your books to the lake?" Michelle asked. "I thought we'd have some of that lasagna from the freezer and a salad, and we could watch a movie—if you get your homework finished first." Roxie stopped, groaned a little, and then slapped her bare feet across the tiled floor to get her book bag, left in the kitchen. "Okay. What movie?"

"Your choice."

"Good deal." She got her bag and trudged back up the stairs.

Michelle turned back to Max. "Anyway, I was thinking. What do you think about having Paul over for dinner? Next week sometime. Maybe if I could be around him away from the gallery in a relaxed home-like atmosphere, I could be more comfortable with him."

"Sure. But what bothers you about him?"

"He's just so—so perfect all the time, and I guess that's intimidating. Always looks perfect, talks perfect. Nobody is that perfect. Nobody."

Max smiled at her. Michelle was always distracted about something, as long as it was something not in her immediate environment. He watched her pour another glass of wine; she was frowning, thinking now about the new director of the gallery. Sometimes he wanted to point out that she was always distracted, but he feared it would sound like a complaint, so he said nothing, just as he said nothing about the third glass of wine—when dinner was probably at least a couple hours away.

CHAPTER TWO

Paul Gonzalo Meyer locked his office door on the fourth floor of the prestigious Hunter Gallery, in the fashionable Buckhead section of Atlanta.

He had just turned to head down the dimly-lit corridor toward the elevator, when he noticed a flickering light coming from the janitor's closet in the opposite direction. He thought he should investigate.

When he reached the closet, he stopped in the middle of the corridor and looked through the open door. It was Sofia, an old, Mexican woman who cleaned the offices of the gallery at night. She hadn't heard his approach on the carpeted hallway, so she didn't turn around. She was on her knees facing the sink, sitting back on the heels of worn-out athletic shoes with her head bowed, the gray strands of her unkempt hair pulled back and fastened with a rubberband. She was wearing some kind of dirty, pink sweatsuit, and he could see her bent elbows moving in front of her as she mumbled something softly in Spanish. She was praying her rosary. *El Señor es contigo....* She had placed in the deep sink a large, white candle contained in a soot-stained glass, on which a garish representation of Our Lady of Guadalupe was imprinted. The candle's flickering light caused the glitter-covered rays fanning outward from the figure to move in eerie shadows on the closet's walls, among buckets and brooms in the odorous, dingy darkness.

Paul made an involuntary step backwards. The scene was grotesque. He heard her mumbling again, *"Dios te salve, Maria..."* His lips tightened in a reflex of disgust. He turned and walked rapidly back toward the elevator, away from what he perceived as primitive ignorance, even ugliness. Sofia's

whisper followed him: *El Señor es contigo*.... He passed the
Degas print collection on his way to the elevator. The new
young artist, John Mayfield, was waiting for him at Gino's—all
that was beautiful was waiting for him. He almost ran.

The burlap-covered walls of the elevator further muted its
almost silent operation—he could hear his own rapid
breathing. Soft, indirect lighting illuminated the framed
prints on the elevator walls which advertised past exhibitions
at the gallery. He studied his personal favorite—an ink-on-
watercolor by Elise Johnson, a long-stemmed tiger lily on a
washed ground of deep teal green—and he didn't notice
when his breathing slowed. He felt relaxed and happy as he
walked to his black Mercedes in the parking garage. He was
looking forward to the evening.

He was meeting John Mayfield, a very attractive young
man who had serious talent. It was too late for Hunter to get
his Atlanta debut exhibition; the High already had it lined up
for September, but—and this was important—if Hunter could
get one of his more impressive pieces, it would get twice the
price in October than it would anytime before that first
exhibition. Buyers loved art, but they loved a good
investment even more.

He was humming when he turned the car over to the
parking valet at Gino's. He was about five minutes late.
Perfect. Mayfield would have arrived, if he was on time but
he wouldn't have had to wait more than a minute or two.

Paul was well known at Gino's. He'd been there many
times before he moved to Atlanta to take the job as director
of the Hunter Gallery more than two months ago. He and
Jason, a former lover, used to go to Gino's at least once a
week, every time Paul could get away from the gallery he still
owned in his hometown of Savannah. Jason, a sculptor of
rather mediocre ability, lived in New York now. The affair
had been a long one, almost a year. For a while, Paul actually
thought he might be in love, simply because it was the only
time in his life when he'd had a relationship that lasted more

than a few weeks. But he knew that his attraction was a consequence of Jason's undemanding nature, and the fact that Jason lived in Atlanta; there was enough distance between Atlanta and Savannah to keep the relationship from smothering Paul. In the end, he was glad when Jason moved to New York. Sustained intimacy was not to his liking. Paul was one of those people who had many friends in many different places, from Savannah to Tokyo, and just about every city in between where a really major gallery existed. He liked belonging to everyone, not just one person—which is to say that he liked everyone belonging to him while he himself belonged to no one. He was rather famous, not among the general public, but in the artistic circles where he traveled. Those who knew him personally knew his preference for having no attachments, and if they were ever critical of that trait, they found knowing him to be too valuable to trouble with such minor criticism. Besides, Paul Meyer was a very charming man, as excellent a host as he was a guest, always pleasant, knowledgeable, humorous, and altogether fine company.

"Good evening, Mr. Meyer," the maître d' intoned, "I believe you are meeting someone? He's waiting for you at your favorite table in the lounge. Follow me, please."

They passed a classical Spanish guitarist on a little elevated wooden platform. The plaintive, soulful music seemed almost of place but for a few customers sitting nearby, who were sufficiently appreciative to listen quietly without conversation.

John Mayfield stood to greet him and extended his right hand; his left hand held his glass. "Paul Meyer! It's good to see you."

They shook hands. Paul said he hoped John hadn't waited long and was assured that he'd only just arrived.

His attention went instantly to John's hand—as it always did when he met a painter he really respected, as though the artist's hand was some kind of magical instrument he wanted to examine, to explore in detail. When John lifted his glass to his lips, Paul was surprised and interested to see that he was apparently left-handed.

"A left-handed painter!" he said, smiling. "Now what will the critics make of that?"

John laughed at the remark and said he hoped some critic would have cause to say *anything* concerning him as long as it wasn't negative. Paul said he was certain they would say things—very good things—about John Mayfield. And so the conversation went, but Paul did not squander his flattering remarks about John's work; they were restrained enough to avoid any appearance of insincerity and to keep them valuable when he did offer them. After all, Paul was himself a critic of considerable renown; compliments from him did not come cheap, and any up-and-coming artist would have given a great deal to receive even one.

His drink arrived—bourbon over cracked ice—as well as the menus, which remained unopened while they listened to the suggestions of the chef. Then they mutually agreed that the chateaubriand was an excellent idea, gave their order, and settled into polite, gently exploratory, conversation.

Several things had to be decided: Would Hunter's show John's work? Which piece, or pieces? When? What was the price range they would ask; what percentage would they charge? And finally, would they sleep together that night, and if so, where?

Paul Meyer already knew all the answers to these questions that would be discussed and explored, and would seem to be mutually "decided." Hunter's would show one piece, and he knew which piece. It would be marked "NFS"—not for sale—*before* the High debut, without the artist's name in order to arouse interest in the artist. After the High exhibition, and the reviews Paul anticipated, the artist's name would be posted along with a price that would be determined solely by the impact of the debut. Hunter's would get sixty percent, maybe more, and a commitment for another exhibition,   exclusive to the Hunter Gallery, next spring at an invitingly lower percentage. In fact, the contract was already drawn up in Paul's office with appropriate blanks where figures would go. And finally, yes, they would sleep together that night—in John's room, charged to the High Museum, at the Hyatt Regency. Paul never took anyone home with him.

CHAPTER THREE

Paul welcomed Michelle Maxwell's dinner invitation. He liked her. He knew she'd felt a little resentment when he was hired as director, but not much. She was a good arts administrator, but she knew her limitations; she couldn't compete with his successful gallery in Savannah, still less with his renown as a critic. She had been with the Hunter Gallery a long time, but although she had an excellent record, she had no "name," nor had she ever displayed a competitive instinct or a talent for innovative thinking. Michelle was not an innovator, but a maintainer—a valuable one—and the board recognized that capability. When Paul was brought in as director, she got a salary increase.

Paul admired her good taste as well as her administrative ability. Too often, arts administrators seemed to feel compelled toward a Bohemian appearance and personality. Michelle was a lady, and she both acted and dressed the part. Her clothes were definitely not off the rack, and Paul knew she could hardly afford such a wardrobe on her salary. Discreet inquiry revealed that her husband was a successful attorney and came from old "Decatur money." Probably a minimal income of seven figures, he thought. He was curious to meet her husband and see her home.

It was large—three floors, a garage for multiple vehicles, dark red brick, tucked away among tall trees and hedges on about five lush acres in a very affluent suburb outside Alpharetta. The house looked like solid wealth, understated and comfortable, with an atmosphere of permanence, as though it could survive wars or tornadoes or economic collapses.

A clock somewhere with a Westminster chime sounded when a maid opened the front door to greet him warmly by name. She took the wine he'd brought and led him toward the back of the house to a large, tiled room with a glass wall that overlooked a beautifully landscaped pool. Two or three children were in the pool, swimming, laughing, and playing.

"Paul!" Michelle sprang up from a white leather sofa. "Come in. Good to see you. I'm glad you could come." She was wearing pants of cocoa silk and a magenta blouse, a picture of casual elegance. A man stood up, rather large and serious-looking.

"This is my husband, Max." They shook hands. She made a sweeping gesture toward three other people. "And my mother, Laura. She's visiting us this weekend from St. Augustine. And this is my brother, George, and his wife, Carolyn. They brought her up to see us. Have a seat. What can I get you to drink?"

He nodded and smiled, then settled into an overstuffed chair facing the others. "Whatever you're having will be fine."

"Well," said Max, heading for the bar, set up on a sideboard. "I'm having bourbon. Will that do?"

"Perfectly. Just a little ice, please." Was that a Chagall painting above the sideboard? He couldn't resist; he had to look closer. He got up and stood by Max, pouring his drink. Paul peered closer at the canvas. "Michelle, is this really a Chagall?"

"Indeed it is. A wedding present from my father."

"Lucky you." He sat back down with his drink and noticed then that the entire room had been decorated to complement the painting. The picture's muted browns and blues were surrounded by soft blue textures, brown pillows, and white tile.

Dinner surprised him. Roast beef, mashed potatoes, peas and carrots, served family style, with the children at the same table with the adults. No gourmet menu; no servant waiting at table. They had coffee afterward back in the family room, the children relegated to their own playroom downstairs.

The conversation covered politics—Michelle's brother dominated that topic—as well as gardening, the major contributors there being Laura and her daughter-in-law, Carolyn.

Everyone expressed polite interest in Paul's background and his gallery in Savannah, which, it turned out, had been patronized by George and Carolyn on more than one occasion. Michelle's husband was rather quiet, almost noticeably withdrawn. Paul asked him what kind of law he practiced, and his reply, "estate planning," gave him an idea.

"I wonder if I could talk to you about a matter I've been intending to deal with for some time now."

"Certainly," Max answered. "You're a single man, right? Are you concerned, maybe, about your parents?"

"No. My mother—well, I'll put it this way: she needs no help from me. Neither does my father. My parents have been divorced since I was a small child. He's been remarried for many years now with another family in California. No—it's my grandmother I'm thinking about."

"Wow, Paul, she must be quite elderly. You're lucky to have her still with you." Michelle joined in. "How old is she?"

"She's eighty. She has a little trouble now, a mild case of dementia. She's my father's mother, and I'm afraid he sort of forgot to take care of a few things on her behalf. The divorce wasn't an amiable one, and my mother—though she could easily afford to do it—hasn't felt an inclination to take responsibility there." He smiled a little uncomfortably; he didn't like having to share such personal information. "Anyway, I guess it falls to me. I'm her only grandchild."

Max sensed his discomfort. "Well, I'm sure we can work out whatever you feel you need to do. Let me go get you a card." He left the room and returned with a business card. "Just call me when you want to discuss it."

"Thanks," said Paul. "I'll call Monday and get an appointment."

* * *

That night, Paul drove back into the city thinking about the evening. It was so—*family*. Just briefly, he wondered if Michelle had intended to show him this, to show what he was missing. But no, that wasn't her—she had no meanness about her. No, she'd wanted, probably, simply to be more comfortable in her relationship with him, and she'd thought that sharing her home and family with him would bring that about. If so, it worked. He already felt closer to her, as though he knew her better now, and he liked her even more for it.

Family made him think of his own family. His mother traveled constantly, even more than he did, and their relationship, though friendly and affectionate, was not a close one. There had been no contact with his father in years, and he fought down an impulse to old anger now, not for his father's abandonment of him—that was long ago—but for his father's neglect of his own mother. Except for Paul, Nana was alone.

His grandmother lived in a condominium in Savannah that he bought for her, but her declining mental capabilities made it clear to him that other arrangements should be made now. She reverted to her native Spanish more and more. That wasn't a problem in itself. But it meant something—he wasn't sure what—and she looked so wistful sometimes. He decided to phone her doctor Monday, before he called Maxwell's office.

* * *

"Well," asked Max, "What do you think? Think he enjoyed himself? He seemed to."

Michelle's mother and the children went to bed, and the four adults sat in the family room having a nightcap together before going to bed themselves. George and Carolyn were leaving from the airport the next morning for a few days in New York. Their two children, along with Laura, were to stay with Max and Michelle; the parents would pick them up on their return, taking Laura back to her condo in St. Augustine before going home to Gainesville, Florida. George was a professor of American history at the university there.

"Well, if he didn't, he sure was good at faking it," answered George. "Why does he have dark features? With a name like Meyer, you'd think he would look more Germanic."

"I don't know," said Carolyn, "but he's certainly good-looking. Wow."

"Yes, he is," said Michelle. "And he's so blooming perfect, isn't he? In appearance—perfect hair, skin, even perfect teeth. And he's always perfectly dressed. But even his manner, his personality, is—" she laughed. "He's even got a designer personality."

Max felt a little defensive on behalf of their guest. "My God, Michelle, are you going to fault somebody for being perfect?"

"No, I'm not. Just got to accept that, I guess. The main thing is—yes, I do think he enjoyed himself, whether he was faking it or not. And I will feel more relaxed around him now. Just get past his perfectness and take it for real. I think we'll have a little more—what should I call it—a little more unguardedness now. I'm glad y'all liked him. He really is a nice guy." For Michelle, the evening was a success.

"Didn't you say he was gay?" asked Carolyn. "He didn't look like a gay man."

Max laughed at her. "What's a gay man supposed to look like, Carolyn?"

CHAPTER FOUR

Paul's secretary buzzed him: "It's a man who says his name is Dr. Hernandez. Do you want to pick up?"

"Thanks, Lolly, I've got it." Paul pressed the button for incoming calls. "Good morning, Doctor. Thanks for returning my call so quickly. I know how busy your schedule is."

"That's all right, Mr. Meyer. What can I do for you?"

"Well, I talked to you before about my grandmother's dementia, and I've started to wonder if it's time to think about some help for her—like a live-in companion, maybe? Or do you think she should go to an assisted living facility? The reason I'm asking now is that I'm going to see an attorney about some financial arrangements for her, and I need to think about what kind of needs she might have, both now and in the future."

"That's probably a good idea. To tell you the truth, she seems to be holding her own right now, but that's not to say the dementia won't progress—it will. Just a speculative projection—I'd say that assisted living is a year or so away. For now, the home-health service reports that she's doing okay on her own. Of course, that could change any time—and without much warning."

"Is there any way of estimating the costs for the facility?" Paul grabbed a pencil and notepad. He knew he wouldn't get any exact figures, but anything approaching an estimate would be helpful.

"That depends on the facility you choose, of course," replied Dr. Hernandez. "Just going by the standards you've set already, however, I think you should look at the possibility of six or seven thousand."

"Wow. Not cheap, is it?" Paul scribbled some notes in

addition to the figure: *insurance? trust fund?* He also had to
think about taking care of her if something happened to him.

"No, indeed it's not."

"Okay. Thanks, Doctor. This helps me get started. I can
ask the attorney about other issues. And thanks again for
calling."

"No problem." The doctor hung up. Paul deliberately put
aside any further thought about it, knowing that he could not
guess actual costs until he talked to Maxwell.

Michelle came in with the proposed budget to present at
the next board meeting. "Have you got time to deal with this
now, Paul?"

"Sure. Come on in. And by the way, thanks again for the
other night. You have a beautiful home and family. Thanks
for sharing it with me." He stood and moved toward the
conference table at the other end of the room.

"Oh, it was our pleasure, believe me. I'm sorry my son,
Jacob, wasn't there. He has aspirations to be an artist." She
smiled. "Maybe a good thing he wasn't there—he would have
wanted to show you some of his work."

They settled into chairs at the table, poured some coffee,
and spread out the budget. Paul estimated it would take at
least an hour, so he buzzed Lolly to ask her to see that they
weren't disturbed. The board meeting was only two days
away; the budget had to be finalized now.

* * *

Shortly after lunch, Max's secretary, JoAnn, asked Paul to
hold the line a moment, then buzzed Max to ask if he
wanted to take on a new client—a Paul Meyer was calling for
an appointment. Max told her he'd take the call.

"Morning, Paul. I didn't expect you to call this soon.
When would you like to talk about this?"

"As soon as possible, Max. I just had a conversation with
my grandmother's doctor this morning. Sounds like
something should be set up fairly soon."

"Well, nothing's open on the office calendar for some time. Why don't you let me take you to lunch—say, tomorrow."

"That would be great, Max. I could tell you what I know now, and you could tell me what's possible, maybe give me a few options to think about. I think I need to decide something pretty quickly, even if it's not going to be operational, so to speak, for a while." He wanted to get matters settled. The doctor's comments had made the situation a little more urgent than he'd thought.

"Do you know Lombardi's on Tenth Street? It's not far from the gallery. Michelle and I meet for lunch there sometimes. If that's okay, how about one o'clock? After the lunch rush."

"It's fine. I'll see you there tomorrow at one. And thanks, Max."

* * *

Paul took a walk through the gallery after the call. He did that every day, but he tried to vary the time for the sake of security—though the small staff thought he varied it to keep them on their toes. Each of the gallery's three floors open to the public had its own information desk with a representative, but there was only one security guard, who remained at the entrance door. Hunter's had a few pieces priced in six figures. There was an alarm system, but security was still a concern.

The Hunter Gallery was established some forty years ago through an endowment from the Marvin S. Hunter Foundation, for the purpose of encouraging new artists. Since that time, it became a fixture in Atlanta arts society. More than a few artistic careers were launched by the Hunter Gallery. In the past several years, however, the gallery was less inclined to risk-taking; just about every exhibition now included the works of established artists only, making the

gallery less profitable as well as less authoritative. Paul hoped
to change that.

Today he wanted to decide where the John Mayfield
piece would go. The right location was important, not least
because the piece he'd chosen to show was huge. It would
dominate any location in the gallery, but because it would
not be for sale yet, and because its signature would be
covered, pending John's debut elsewhere, it shouldn't be on
the main floor. He decided on the central wall of the
mezzanine.

As always, he chatted with the gallery representative on
each floor. He wanted to know how many visitors there had
been, what questions were asked, what answers were given,
and most of all, how many serious inquiries had been
made—were there potential buyers? He collected cards and
phone numbers left, and amended each of them according
to the representative's comments. It had been a good
morning: There were inquiries about several items, none of
them listed at less than a thousand. At the mezzanine, he
told the representative that a new work would go on the
central wall. It would be NFS and the artist was to remain
unknown, but he wanted her to note especially how many
viewers the piece would get, what questions were asked about
it—in short, she was to note the reaction to the piece, due to
go up tomorrow before the board meeting.

For the rest of his hour-long tour, he enjoyed the gallery.
The new skylights he had ordered to be installed on the
sloping front side of the third floor gave particular emphasis
to the requirements for light and shadow of sculpture—always
exhibited in the curved "S" walls in the center of the floor. It
was quite successful; he was pleased. One of the smaller
paintings on the back wall was a Spanish landscape,
particularly lovely. It was a communal well in Majorca with
women washing laundry, talking to each other animatedly; it
brought his grandmother to mind—and Spain.

His grandmother was born in Barcelona. She married an

American Navy officer after the Second World War and came to the United States—to Savannah—to await his return from sea duty. But he never returned. Paul's grandfather died while he was on duty in the Pacific, not long after she gave birth to Nathaniel, Paul's father. Nana had not returned to Spain then as she might have been expected to do. She stayed in the country of her husband's birth and her son's. She spoke English very well, became a teacher in a Catholic school in Savannah, and raised her son. She never remarried. She took her son to Spain every two years so he could meet the other members of his family in Barcelona and learn Spanish language and culture.

Paul frowned and his face darkened as he remembered how his father talked about these childhood visits to Spain with a groan—as though he were not only burdened with a foreign mother, but also with a kind of mandatory requirement that he become "foreign" as well. Knowing how much her son hated spending his summers in Spain, she stopped taking him there when he was around twelve. And because he wanted to stay in the United States, she stayed too. She never returned to Spain after that.

But there was no need to remember this now. Actually, he pondered what he came to think of as the "Barcelona coincidence:" a major national gallery there had offered him a position around the same time he'd received the offer from the Hunter Gallery, and he'd taken the Hunter offer precisely because it would allow him to stay near his grandmother. Certainly, he'd wanted the Barcelona job, though the salary was less than he'd been offered by Hunter's board. He'd visited that magnificent gallery several times and he would have jumped at the chance to work there, but for his Barcelona-born grandmother—who lived now in the United States, in Savannah. Fate, he thought, had a sense of irony.

His cell phone rang. It was John. "Hi. What's going on?"

"Just finishing packing up. I thought I'd see if you

wanted to do dinner before my flight leaves." John was headed back to Kansas City that night. His arrangements with the High Museum had been completed days ago, but he'd stayed on in Atlanta.

"What time does your flight leave?" Paul asked.

"Nine-fifty. I should check in a half-hour before flight time."

"What, that would be kind of pushing it, don't you think?" Paul asked. He knew John wouldn't agree. He'd seen him four times since their meeting at Gino's over a week ago. He didn't like the idea of sentimental farewells, of feeling pressured to visit John in Kansas or inviting him back to Atlanta during the summer before his exhibition in September. It had been pleasant, but it was what it was. "By the way," he said, hoping to divert attention from the subject of dinner, "I've got just the spot for *Coeur de Lion*. I'm standing there now. You know the glass wall on the mezzanine? You'll be able to see it from the first floor. It's on the loading dock—should be up tonight or tomorrow."

There was just a hint of disappointment in John's reply. "Okay. Well, then I guess I'll see you in September."

"Right. Have a good trip. I'll be in touch."

CHAPTER FIVE

Michelle lay in bed a moment or two before opening her eyes, already thinking about the day ahead, oblivious to the crumpled eiderdown held up to her chin with closed fists, to the early summer sunlight around the edges of the drapes, and to Max's slow, steady breathing close to her neck. She turned to look at him, his rumpled brown hair above a face as innocent as a sleeping baby's, and she felt—as she often did when she looked at him without his awareness of it—her heart actually "soften," its beating slowed, its rhythm steadied. It was a physical sensation, accompanied by a relaxation of the muscles around her eyes and mouth. She had the same physical reaction sometimes when she looked at her children.

How sweet of him. He told her last night that he was meeting Paul for lunch today to help him figure out arrangements for his grandmother. Michelle knew that not only was there no room for new clients on Max's calendar, but that none of the estates he managed was worth less than several million. He would do it *pro bono*, she knew, with no charge to Paul. How dear of him. She wondered if Paul had any idea that he was completely unable to afford an attorney of Max's stature. Probably not.

As if he could feel her looking at him, Max opened his eyes and whispered, "Hey there, Priss." It was his childhood nickname for her. She moved the hair from his forehead and kissed it, and then they made love. The way they always did—slowly, tenderly, loving each other, and submitting to the love of each other, accepting it, welcoming it.

Afterward, in the shower, Michelle wondered if their sex life was "healthy." It was never frantic, desperate, or passionate, but rather like an old couple who, disregarding the dance fashion of the day or the music, slide around the floor in the same foxtrot they always danced, part of each other. Was that how they were supposed to be? Was Max content with her and with their lovemaking? She didn't know; she only knew that Max was unspeakably dear to her. She had an appreciation of other men's good looks, but she'd never even thought of infidelity to Max, to her marriage. What about Max, she wondered. Was he ever tempted? He seemed so detached from her and the children sometimes, as though he wasn't really there. Did he crave more excitement, or adventure?

Then she thought of Max's father; he had the same personality. Max once told her back when they were in high school that his father never once kissed him, and it was easy to believe that was true. Max Senior was devoted to his family, but he was thoroughly undemonstrative. Although he never expressed affection physically, and seldom verbally, he was, like Max, generous and open-hearted. And, like Max, that trait made him vulnerable, almost like a child.

* * *

Max found Paul studying the menu at Lombardi's. Paul hadn't seen him approach and stood quickly when he saw him, smiled, and shook his hand. "Oh, hello, Max. You sort of sneaked up on me. Just trying to figure out what's good here. You tell me—you said you eat here often."

Max pulled out a chair and sat down. "Well, depends on your appetite. If you're hungry and you're not a vegetarian, the sausage frittata is pretty good. My favorite, anyway. Michelle likes their seafood pretty well. She usually gets one of those seafood crepes. I have to say, though, if you're a connoisseur, you won't think too much of their wines here."

"I never drink wine with lunch, anyway," Paul replied.

Max's face clouded a little; he wished Michelle could say

that. A waiter appeared at his elbow. "Afternoon, Mr. Maxwell. Can I get you gentlemen anything to drink?"

"Just water for me, please," said Paul, and Max nodded, indicating he'd have the same.

* * *

Later, much later, Max remembered that moment. How could it have been anything so trivial, so frivolous as that? Yet, as if he were using a yardstick, measuring backwards, that was the moment, the real moment it started. A shared preference for water over wine with lunch? Absurd, utterly absurd. Yet it had come right on the heels of his concern about Michelle's drinking—did that have any part in it? And was that "concern" actually a *disapproval* that he'd disguised to himself? The question was too ridiculous. In any case, yes, that was the moment it started.

* * *

Paul liked Max. He liked his conservatism, his lawyer-like dark suit and muted striped tie, his slow, considered questions, and thoughtful responses. But it was something more than his manner—it was his solidity. He knew Max was the ethical rock on which people could build a confidence; he was trustworthy, reliable. He seemed the perfect mate for a woman like Michelle, and he suspected she knew that very well. She would have dominated, unhappily, a lesser man.

He hadn't intended to reveal so much of his background or personal information, but Max made it both safe and easy to do. He didn't ask for details, only for financial information, any pre-existing arrangements Paul might have made, any insurance he might have. Was his grandmother listed as a dependent on Paul's health insurance? Yes. Was his grandmother on Medicare? Yes. Did she have any financial resources of her own? No. Any insurance of her own? Yes, but it was negligible, and so on.

Max asked the questions slowly and deliberately, without any comments of his own. Finally, he frowned, and apparently having put the limited information together, he asked, "Paul, is your grandmother a foreign-born U.S. citizen?"

"Yes. She married an American serviceman while he was on active duty in Spain and returned to the States with him. When he died, she received a pension, which she still gets, but, of course, it's completely inadequate now. I bought her a condo in Savannah near the gallery I have there, but now she has dementia. It's a mild form, but it's progressing. The doctor says she'll need to go to an assisted living facility probably in a year or so. It'll cost around seven thousand a month."

"Can you afford that?"

"On my present income, yes, but not indefinitely, if the cost of the facility goes up—as it's likely to do. But what would happen to her if I lost my job, if my gallery went downhill, if my investments turned sour—what would happen to her if I died?"

"Can you send me a financial statement? Fax it over to the office?"

"Sure. I'll do it this afternoon."

"Okay. But there's one more thing." Max buttered a piece of Lombardi's delicious Italian bread. Paul waited. He had already learned that he could defer to this man, trust him, and that made it easy to be patient.

Finally, Max looked straight into his eyes and asked, "What does she want? You haven't said a word about what your grandmother wants."

* * *

And for Paul, that was it. That was the moment when he began to love Max, though he wouldn't realize it until much later. For now, his face flushed a little, and he smiled almost shyly, embarrassed like a small boy questioned gently by a loving father to make his son aware of some moral matter the son might not have considered.

"No," he said quietly. "I think I've been concerned with doing what's best for her without giving thought to what she might want."

"Well," said Max, putting his knife and fork down on his now-empty plate. "That's the first order of business now, I think. Talk to your grandmother first, and then we'll talk again."

* * *

That afternoon, Max's secretary brought in Paul's fax, and Max studied it briefly. No, Paul could not afford seven thousand a month plus all the other medical expenses his grandmother was likely to incur—not for long, anyway, not without a considerable increase in his own assets. His annual income came to a few hundred thousand. A single man his age could live very comfortably with that—except for the dependency of his grandmother. Not the way Paul wanted her to live, anyway. He looked at the medical expense sheets —high-priced specialists, way beyond what Medicare provided, or what his own supplemental insurance provided. He strongly suspected that Paul was being overzealous in his care for his grandmother and was being exploited by doctors who might not be altogether scrupulous. Did she really need a spiral CT-scan every year, or hospitalization for general tests? Not likely. He had not asked about funeral and burial arrangements—very minor concerns, anyway, he thought, looking at the medical expense recap sheet.

Paul had stayed in the forefront of his mind ever since lunch. He admired him for wanting to take care of his grandmother, though his own suggestions, now beginning to form after looking at the fax, might not be what Paul expected. But what he thought about most was Paul himself.

There was a genuine magnanimity there—an unusual largeness of heart. He knew, however, that he wasn't really *thinking* about him so much as he was *seeing* him, like a piece of music one continues to hear long after the actual sound is gone.

He could see Paul's eyes, so dark they looked almost black, like his hair, brushed back in thick waves. Yet his skin was fair, not olive; in fact, he was almost pale. And Michelle was right: he was "perfect." His features were chiseled, almost like a statue, and perfectly proportioned. He was—he noticed that he didn't even hesitate to use the word— *beautiful.* He remembered George's comment that he didn't look Germanic to match the surname of "Meyer;" now he knew why. No, he looked Spanish. The dark features must have dominated the Meyer features.

And then he remembered Carolyn's remark that Paul didn't look gay. He'd laughed at Carolyn. Now, it seemed like a sober remark, not a comic one. The man was beautiful, the most beautiful man he'd ever seen.

* * *

Michelle waited on the mezzanine with the rest of Hunter's small staff. Paul was personally supervising the unloading of the Mayfield canvas and its transport up the service elevator. She had seen slides of Mayfield's work and even attended a show last year in Philadelphia which included a few of his pieces. She was eager to see *Coeur de Lion.* Paul came down the hallway from the service elevator with two men rolling a large hand-truck with the boarded-up canvas. It looked as big as the wall itself. The men carefully removed the wooden pallet-like boards, and then the Styrofoam sheeting. Everybody, including Paul, seemed stunned by the painting.

"My gosh," said Ann, one of the gallery reps. "It's magnificent!"

Michelle was quiet for a moment as she studied it. "I

don't know what I think. It looks like the center of a giant chrysanthemum!"

Paul laughed. "I wonder what kind of buyer would be interested in it—where they'd hang it."

"Well," said Ann, "after the High exhibition, *somebody* will find a place for it. There are people in Atlanta who'll decide they love it and just have to own it. Wait and see."

"I'm still not sure," Michelle pondered. "And you shouldn't underestimate Atlanta buyers. It might be harder to sell than you think. But it has impact, anyway."

CHAPTER SIX

For once, the main topic of the board's conversation was herself, which seemed to please her, even though it made her somewhat nervous. Since this was only his second board meeting, he had only one to compare it with, but Michelle said they never accepted a proposed budget that quickly before—only a few questions had been asked, and the answers were evidently quite satisfactory. The budget was accepted unanimously after a discussion of just fifteen minutes or so. Michelle was delighted; she was also rather pleased, it seemed to Paul, to be allowed to do the presentation, instead of merely being on hand to answer questions.

But it was the Mayfield painting that dominated their conversation. Each of the members had seen it before the meeting, not on an organized tour of the gallery—that never happened—but they knew about the High exhibition in September, and about Paul's plan to show the painting right away. They were curious. Several members had seen Mayfield's work before, and there was considerable discussion of how this painting departed from his earlier work, yet how it also seemed to draw on the best of the artist's native expressionism, softened by a new impressionistic kind of realism. Paul wasn't surprised by the enthusiasm; after all, the board members were all devoted fans of visual art, but he was more gratified by their equally enthusiastic approval of his plan to show the painting ahead of the exhibition, not for sale until afterwards. They didn't just approve of the painting itself, but of *him* also. One of the reasons Paul was good at pleasing people was that he enjoyed it so much—he liked to please, especially those in authority.

He was seated now on the sofa in his living room, bare

feet up on the large square coffee table in front of him, a beer in one hand and remote control in the other, viewing a slideshow sent to him from his gallery in Savannah. He intended to drive down there in the morning; he had to talk to his grandmother, as Max had instructed him to do. And it was Max who was on his mind, not the pottery he viewed on the slides. He could see him so clearly, his butter knife poised above a piece of bread, looking at Paul quite—*directly* seemed the best word to describe it—firmly directing Paul's attention to something that had not occurred to him, that he should have done and had not. The unexpectedness of Max's look, as much as the question that accompanied it, caught him off-guard—when he didn't even know he'd been on-guard. It made him feel exposed and vulnerable, and aware of the fact, for the first time, that he had been guarded. Was it just when the subject of conversation was his grandmother, or was he always guarded?

His imagination shifted, or expanded then, and he saw Michelle next to Max, and their two children with them: charming little Roxanne, and the artist-son Jacob, whom he'd never seen. *How blessed you all are*, he thought to himself, *to have him;* to the artist-son, he said, *to have his fatherhood. Do any of you know how blessed you are?*

He reached for his cell phone on the coffee table and pressed the speed-dial button for his grandmother's number. The phone rang three times before she answered. He always worried if it rang more than twice, though he knew his anxiety wasn't justifiable.

"Hola," she answered. It was the first time she'd ever answered the phone in Spanish. He wasn't sure that was a good sign.

"Hi, Nana. It's me. How are you?"

"Oh, *querido,* it's so good to hear from you! Are you all right? I'm fine, honey, just fine. Is everything okay?"

"Yes, dear, everything's great. I just wanted to tell you I'm driving down there tomorrow morning. Will you be at home?"

"Oh, that's wonderful. Of course, I'll be here—I'm always here. What time?"

"Probably around eleven. Hey, I'll take you out to lunch, okay?"

"Very okay, dear."

"Great. I'll see you tomorrow. Be thinking about where you want to go for lunch. I love you." He rang off. She sounded okay, he thought, but wondered how much she'd reverted to Spanish, whether she'd started to think in Spanish. He wished he'd remembered to ask her doctor if the reversion to her native language was symptomatic, a sign that the dementia was progressing.

He made another quick call to Peg Litchfield, who managed the Meyer Gallery in Savannah, to let her know he was coming tomorrow afternoon.They talked briefly about which pieces of the pottery they should offer for sale, considering the ones he viewed on the slides. Peg was really good at displaying three-dimensional art—something Paul considered an art form in itself—and he left all decisions about display up to her.

* * *

The long, boring drive to Savannah the next morning on Interstate 16 was unusually miserable. He tried listening to satellite radio, to audiobooks, but nothing helped. He finally gave up attempts at diversion and allowed his meandering thoughts to surface instead.

Nana. Her small, graceful bone structure was so different from her son's big, burly frame. Paul thought that his father must have inherited only his grandfather's genes; there was nothing of Nana in his appearance or in his personality. She was soft-spoken, gentle, and had that ability to—to *pay attention.* How odd it was that she should be so gifted in the very quality that his father lacked so completely. He had very little memory of his parents' divorce—he'd been only about four years old—but it was easy to understand its cause; he never needed to ask. Not without affection, he thought his mother might very well be the vainest person he'd ever known, male or female. Attention, for her, was air to breathe—much more important than love. The divorce had never been a mystery. What he sometimes wondered was why his mother had been attracted to a man like his father, a man who seemed incapable of paying attention to anyone except himself. Maybe because they were alike, in a way.

My family is certainly not like Max's, he thought. *But*...he glanced at his long, slender fingers on the steering wheel, but...*well, it's the one I have, I guess. Some things we don't get to choose.*

Nana was his family. He was fond of his mother, amused by her; he was indifferent to his long-absent father, who simply didn't matter. Nana was his heart. Yet it was only Nana who knew nothing—as far as he knew, anyway about his homosexuality. He'd told his mother when he was a teenager. She hugged him—she often hugged him—but then she hugged everybody.

"Oh, Paulie, yes, dear, I know." It might have been an announcement rather like a decision to be a vegetarian, dutifully acknowledged, accepted, but not ultimately very relevant.

He'd told his father when he finished graduate school. Why did he tell him? Now—for the first time, really—Paul thought his *reason* for telling his father might be more important than his father's reaction. Why had he told him? He knew his father had little interest in him anyway. Was he trying to shock him, maybe even hurt him somehow?

"Oh? Well," his father replied, "whatever floats your boat. God—that sounds terrible, doesn't it?" And he laughed. Then he clapped his arm around Paul's shoulder, as if they were old chums, and said, "Well, I mean, if that's the way things are, son, I guess that's the way things are." And he changed the subject.

He'd never told Nana. Why? Because she would be disappointed in him or disapprove? No. He didn't tell her because *she would have paid attention.* She would have asked questions—pertinent questions. She'd want to know things, details, things he didn't want to tell her.

Paul had known he was gay since his early teens, probably before then. Even if he disregarded the pubescent fantasies, he had to notice when he found boys more interesting than girls in high school. And it wasn't long until everybody else noticed his lack of interest in girls and drew their own conclusions. On the whole, he had a rather easy time of it. He lived in New York with his mother at the time, and the students at the private school he attended in Manhattan were much more sophisticated than they might have been somewhere else. Besides, many of them had same-sex attractions themselves—or thought they did. It was fashionable. He was popular with both sexes; some of the gay boys came on to him from time to time, but he remained a virgin until his senior year.

He'd taken an early-admission class at the Savannah School of Art and Design that year and lived with his grandmother in the house on Baedlin Avenue, where his father grew up and where he spent summers as a child. He loved that little house—in fact, he loved Savannah, with its great oaks and Spanish moss, its warm tangy smell, and good food. And he liked the people—their slow, relaxed culture. It was one of the few places in the United States where art made no class distinctions. New Yorkers pretended to something that came as easy as breathing to both millionaires and housemaids in Savannah. His grandmother had retired from teaching at St. Vincent's Academy, so she was able to go to Mass every day at St. Rose of Lima, the Catholic Church which was only two blocks from her house. When he didn't have a class, Paul went with her. He remembered now, walking to church with her that day, past the black, wrought-iron fences in front of tiny gardens of the narrow houses on Baedlin Avenue. The heat that day was unusually oppressive. The river, a mile away, smelled bad. There was an air that day that was hard to breathe, an air that smelled, and covered the city with a sense of something corrupt and inescapable.

CHAPTER SEVEN

When Savannah was founded in 1769, it was laid out in squares, a situation that suited its expected growth admirably, but its founders had not anticipated modern automobiles. One-way traffic made the historic district a little more difficult to navigate than it would have been in 1769. Still, Paul always drove by the old house on Baedlin Avenue on his way to his grandmother's condominium. He had no idea what his grandfather paid for the little house so long ago, but he was certain it was far less than the 250,000 dollars it brought five years ago. It was situated just inside the historic district, in a fashionable neighborhood of well-maintained historic residences.

Paul had used the income from the house and put 200,000 dollars of his own money with it, raised by mortgaging the gallery, to buy his grandmother a luxurious condominium overlooking the river. The condo was, she insisted, far too large for her. And she was horrified by the cost of its professional decoration. Paul wondered now if he'd done the right thing for her. Would she really have been happier with something smaller, less expensive? He could almost hear Max asking, "What does *she* want? Have you asked her?" The decorator was very good—patient with Nana, and accommodating. She'd spent days just talking to Nana—she, at least, had been concerned with what Nana wanted.

The beautiful rose-gold color of the old brick of Number Eleven Baedlin Avenue, mellow now in the late morning sunlight, warmed his heart, made him smile. Very little had changed. The new owners had installed historically correct working shutters, creamy white, with little wrought-iron handles, and a beveled-glass front door, but everything else was the same. He drove past the corner of Devlin Street, where he would have turned if he drove directly to the condo. But he went a block out of his way in order to avoid driving by St. Rose of Lima Catholic Church. He didn't want to feel that coldness that gathered around his heart whenever he was forced to go there by some circumstance or other.

The coldness was not caused by fear. On the contrary, it was a kind of deadness. Nana was a devout Catholic; she never missed Sunday Mass, nor would she allow Paul to miss Mass when he lived with her through those long summers when he was growing up. Now, she went to Mass at a church close to the condo, but he still remembered his days at St. Rose's as an acolyte, with his grandmother in the front pew, watching him with loving eyes.

And he still remembered Father Murphy. He remembered too well. The old watery blue eyes boring into his back in the sacristy, the fumbling hands pretending to adjust the hood-collar of his alb, the breath on the back of his neck. And he remembered the old man's clammy skin, his twitching smile, and his whimpering pleading.

That was the worst part of it all. It was his first sexual experience, but the old priest assumed that Paul hadn't known before that experience that he was gay. And Paul let him believe that. And so he watched him with that coldness growing inside him as the priest covered his face with his skinny old hands, cried, and begged to be forgiven. And the coldness grew. "I've turned you queer!" the priest cried stupidly in his thick Irish brogue. Paul said nothing, just watched him from across the small office next to the sacristy, his face frozen in contempt.

He was still amazed sometimes by how easily he'd hidden the incident from his grandmother. She'd never suspected a thing. They still went to Mass—though he stopped doing his altar duty—and he watched as Nana, smiling, shook the priest's hand at the doorway afterwards. A few years ago, she'd said to him, "Oh, Paul—guess what? You remember

Father Murphy at St. Rose's? Well, he died last week, but the terrible thing is—Paul, he committed suicide!"

"That's too bad, dear. Sorry to hear it."

"But, Paul—suicide is a mortal sin!" she answered, and tears welled up in her eyes. And every year, on the anniversary of his death, she paid a stipend to have a Mass said for poor old Father Murphy's soul.

For some reason then, he changed his mind and doubled back to go by St. Rose's after all. There would be a new priest now, anyway, and he was curious to see the inside of the little church again. He pulled into a parking space that happened to be open right in front of the church, got out of the car and went through the wide double doors into the dark interior—always cool, even without air conditioning. He almost dipped his fingers into the holy water font by the door, but he caught himself. He didn't sit down, just walked around, looking at the dark mellow wood of the pews, polished by years of human touch; the marble floor, cracked and filled in a checkered pattern; and the windows, narrow and tall, in a kaleidoscope of colors that seemed almost alive, windows that he'd thought were so beautiful when he was a child.

It was just a small neighborhood church, not an important one, either historically or aesthetically—not listed in any Savannah guidebook. Unpretentious. He looked again at the vivid windows, remembering each one. Because the church was small, the windows served as the fourteen Stations of the Cross, seven on each side of the little sanctuary, each scene depicting a sorrow on the *Via Dolorosa*. He'd loved those windows when he was a child. And then the Crucifix, hanging above the ornate brass tabernacle behind the small marble altar. It was wood, painted in gold. He had thought it magnificent as a child; now, it was just tawdry. He forgot everything else, everything but the inside of the church, seeing it not in its smallness, its present shabbiness, but through the eyes of his childhood. And something occurred

to him then that startled him: *This was it. This was where he
first knew that he loved beauty.* The realization stunned him
for a moment, and he left a little hurriedly, walking past the
closed door of the sacristy without turning to look at it.

* * *

"Paul! Hello, darling." His grandmother hugged him at
the door. She moved aside to let him in, still graceful despite
her eighty years.

"How's my favorite grandmother?"   He hugged her back,
with a little more care than he used to hug her; she was much
frailer now.

"Come sit down, dear. You don't have a bag? You're not
going to stay, are you, Paul? Oh, honey, you can't drive back
to Atlanta today. You should have planned to stay overnight.
After all, isn't that why this place needed a guestroom? At
least, that's what you told me."

"Well, Nana, I do have a job, you know. In fact, I need to
go by Meyer's and see Peg about a few things, too. Let's
don't dally, okay? Because I do have to drive back tonight.
Do you know where you want to have lunch?"

"Where do you think? The Cove, of course. You know
how I love their crab cakes." Her eyes twinkled a little
mischievously. "And a small glass of Chardonnay to go with
them."

"Oh, now, Nana. Does Dr. Hernandez know about that?"

"He doesn't have to know everything, does he? He's not
my father, you know." And suddenly the charmingly
mischievous look vanished and she looked sad.

Paul noticed and knew instantly, instinctively somehow,
that it was the mention of "father" that saddened her. Her
own family members were all gone now—or were they? He
didn't know, and he doubted whether she knew herself.
She'd given up her own family, like a sacrifice, for the sake
of her son. But he said, "Nana, it's a matter of medication.

You know that, don't you? You are taking your medications, aren't you?"

She answered slowly, "Oh, well, yes," as she distractedly sought her handbag and the sweater she always carried when she went out. He knew she wasn't always taking her meds. He just knew it; she was forgetting. And if she was forgetting, she could also forget how *much* of the medication to take. This was serious.

He put his arm around her shoulders and led her through the door. "We need to talk, Nana." He felt grim.

* * *

The long return drive to Atlanta that night needed no diversion from his thoughts, which actually were questions weighing heavily on his furrowed brow — one question, really: what to do.

What *could* he do? He didn't need a doctor to tell him now that Nana could no longer live alone. And a live-in companion was insufficient; any live-in would have to be a nurse, at least, and eventually a nurse would be insufficient as well. She needed to be looked after by a medical staff, with medical equipment available around the clock. It was time— maybe past time—for assisted living.

Seven thousand a month. God! *That's a lot of money*, he thought. Unless he could sell the condo, he didn't know how he'd manage it. Even if he sold it, how long would that revenue last? The gallery was still under mortgage. His conference with Peg that afternoon did not show any great increase in receipts, and he couldn't raise prices without losing patrons. Meyer's was big, it was reputable, but he could lose customers fast by inflating prices. The gallery could be ruined by that kind of thing.

But even as he fretted, mentally arguing one impossible solution over another, at the back of his mind, he remembered asking Nana at The Cove, carefully but bluntly, as Max would have wanted: "Nana, what do you want, darling?"

She put her fork down and looked up at him across the table as if she'd been "caught;" almost like a child, caught in the revelation of some guilty secret—contrite, but knowing it would do no good to be less than honest. Her face, sad and a little fearful, touched his heart.

"Dear," she began hesitantly, then with a gentle determination, "I want to go home."

And he knew she didn't want to go back home to the condo. She wanted to go home—to Spain.

CHAPTER EIGHT

"Max, let's go to church this weekend when Jake comes home." Michelle was buttering a piece of toast.

"Okay." Max was reading the headlines on his laptop.

"Jake's coming home, Jake's coming, bob dee bob!" Roxanne was using her spoon against her cereal bowl like a drum.

"Oh, please, Roxie, stop that!" said Michelle. "And listen, on that topic, don't monopolize his time, okay? He has friends he'd like to see too, you know."

"I don't monopolize him!" Roxie protested, too loudly for any further concentration on the news for Max.

He closed the laptop. "Okay, okay. Are you ready to go? Where's your book bag?"

"I'm taking her this morning, remember?" said Michelle. "You can have some peace with your coffee now—but you get to put the dishes in the dishwasher. Get your bag, Roxie, let's go."

But instead of peace, confusion took over. Gladys the maid arrived, greetings followed, interrupted by a call from his office. Then Roxanne couldn't find her book bag; it was found behind the chair by the door where she'd left it. Michelle kissed the top of his head, Roxie, his cheek, and swift farewells followed. And only then was Max able to get off the phone.

"Good grief," said Gladys, pouring herself a cup of coffee.

"Indeed," replied Max, with some sarcasm. "Listen, you put the dishes in the dishwasher. I'm out of here." He grabbed his jacket from the back of the chair, slipped the laptop in his briefcase and heard Gladys say "Have a nice day!" as he went through the door.

Driving into the city, he remembered Michelle saying they should go to church this weekend. He supposed so. They were tithing-but-seldom-attending members of Christ Church Episcopal. It had probably been two months, so, yes, he supposed they should go. It was good for the kids—and it was the right thing to do, anyway. People, especially families, he thought, should have church in their lives. And there his interest in religion pretty much ended.

His cell rang. Paul's number showed on the screen, and he pressed the speaker button. "Morning! How are you?"

"Hi, Max. Hope I didn't catch you at a bad time. Are you driving?"

"Yes, but it's okay—we're on speaker. What can I do for you?"

"I went to see Nana, my grandmother, yesterday."

Max thought Paul had certainly wasted no time. "You drove all the way down to Savannah and back?"

"Yes. I really want to get this taken care of. Any chance we could talk pretty soon?" Paul had slept little the night before. His concern deepened whenever he thought of Nana's attitude toward her medications.

"Sure. I'm tied up for lunch today, though. Want to have a drink this evening?"

"That would be great."

"Okay, you name the place. I picked the place for lunch."

"Do you know Gino's, off Pearl Street in Northside?"

"Yes, I know where it is. How about five o'clock?"

"I'll see you then. Thanks, Max."

Max thought he'd better let Michelle know he'd be late now, while he was thinking about it. He pressed the button for her number.

"Hey," she answered. He could hear Roxanne singing in the background. "What's up?"

"I'm going to be late this evening. Paul just called me—wants to talk about his grandmother, so we're having a drink at five. I guess you know he went to Savannah yesterday."

"Yes, I knew about that. What time will you be home?"

"I don't know," he replied. "Shouldn't be too long—maybe 6:30. I should be there for dinner."

"Okay. Love you." Then Roxanne squealed: "Hi, Daddy!" just as Michelle hung up. He opened the glove compartment in the car where he kept a pack of cigarettes and lit up. There would be time to get the smell out of the car before Michelle was in it again. She knew he smoked, but he avoided giving occasions for protest. He inhaled deeply and blew the smoke through the lowered window. The rest of the day went smoothly for Max; he looked forward to meeting Paul at Gino's all day long.

* * *

When Paul hung up the phone, he opened his email. Some kind of glitch made transmission stop in the middle of an email from Peg. It was the beginning of a day full of interruptions, with questions he couldn't answer glibly, with thoughts that refused to stay on track to deal with the business at hand. How could he afford what Nana needed?

And, of course, he couldn't give her what she really wanted—to go back to Spain. That couldn't even be considered, and he was afraid she wouldn't be able to understand why.

Michelle noticed his irritable attitude. She thought it must be due to whatever he discovered in Savannah about his grandmother's situation, and decided against asking him about it. Max would find out all about it when they had a drink together that night, and she'd find out from him when he came home.

* * *

Paul sat in his customary seat at Gino's, in the leather armchair by the window, distracted, fiddling with the plastic stirrer in his drink. He didn't notice Max as he entered and approached the little laminated table between the two arm chairs, so he was surprised to look up and see him standing there. He seemed as tall as a mountain, and just about as solid. Dark suit and tie again. And Paul had that feeling again of safety—of being somehow safe in his presence. His worry vanished, he felt calm, secure, even comfortable, for the first time since he left Savannah.

"Hi, Max. Thanks for coming. Have a seat." He gestured toward the other chair. And then it happened. Just as he raised his hand to signal a waiter, Max's hand extended toward the chair. Their hands didn't actually touch, but the air between them turned to velvet. Paul felt a sudden clutch inside him somewhere, as though he'd gasped, unintentionally. He felt himself exhale as Max sat down, looking at him with a little frown, a slight confusion in his eyes.

"No problem. I could use a drink anyway—without the kids, I mean. Jake is supposed to be at home by now. Caught a ride with a friend and came home for the weekend. Roxie's over the moon."

"They're close, huh?"

"Bread and butter." The waiter arrived and he ordered bourbon with ice. "So—what did you find out in Savannah? How's your grandmother? You call her 'Nana,' right?"

"It's not good. Assisted living—the sooner, the better. Dr. Hernandez didn't know about her too-casual attitude toward her medications when I talked to him." He heard the strumming of a guitar chord, followed by soft applause. The Spanish guitarist was back. He felt a bitter taste somewhere in the back of his throat. "Christ, Max. You told me to find out what she wants. She wants to go back to Spain!"

"Uh-oh."

"Yeah. I wish I hadn't asked now."

Max's drink arrived. He sipped it and sucked his teeth a moment. "Well," he began slowly, "does she have any family left there? I mean, if that's what she wants—"

"I believe she has some nieces or nephews. But they don't know her, and she doesn't know them. No. I'm all the family she has."

"Okay. Any chance you'd—?" He held his breath, suddenly very fearful of the answer he might hear. *Paul couldn't leave Atlanta. He wouldn't, would he?* Paul looked so vulnerable sitting there across from him, looking down at the stirrer he was twirling in his long, slender hands. His thick, black lashes lay against cheeks that looked like ivory silk. He did not look like a child; yet, he made Max feel that he was looking at an amazingly beautiful child. He'd never had a response like this to anyone before, man, woman—or child. The near touch of Paul's hand had left him feeling breathless.

"No! Good grief, no. It's out of the question. Even if those nieces and nephews could be found, they wouldn't feel any sense of responsibility for her. She's had no contact with her family since—well, since my father said he didn't want her to." He hadn't meant to be so personal, but it seemed unavoidable. "It's been—what—probably over forty years now since she was in Spain. Besides, she's an American citizen now; she has no claim to any health care in Spain. And none of that is the main reason. How the hell could an eighty-year-old woman just pull up stakes and go to another country *alone?*"

Max sighed with relief. "Well, then, there's no way, is there? I mean, maybe you could take her there for a visit— she'd enjoy that, I'm sure—but not to stay."

"Yes. That's an idea. She might not even want to stay then." *But Nana had said, "I want to go home." And he knew she meant it.*

They finished their drinks. Max asked if Paul wanted another and raised two fingers toward the waiter. "Right.

Well, here's what I've come up with." He leaned down to open the top of his briefcase and get out some notes he'd made after studying Paul's financial statement.

They discussed his options—a will, of course, that would name his grandmother as beneficiary of his estate and naming Max as executor, but past that, there was a good deal of discussion about how to raise money for the assisted living facility. Max reached into his breast pocket and got out his pen; he starting writing figures on the notes. Paul leaned forward, studying the notes. There were question marks next to items like "health insurance premium." He reached behind him to his khaki blazer, thrown over the back of his chair and got his own pen out of the pocket to supply missing figures like deductibles and supplementals. Each of them was aware of their efforts to avoid touch, efforts that finally became awkwardly obvious.

Paul fell backward in his chair, his eyes downcast. Max stopped writing, stopped talking. He put the cap on his pen And sat in the heavy silence that surrounded them both. Paul's face was even paler than usual; he was afraid—afraid he knew what was happening, but certain that Max did not.

Max's cell rang. It was Michelle. "Damn!" he said, looking at his watch. "It's 6:45. I told Michelle I'd be home by 6:30." He pushed his notes back into his briefcase and rose to leave. "I've got to go now. We'll finish this later."

CHAPTER NINE

Roxanne was dozing against Max's left shoulder. He remembered dozing off in church when he was a child; his mother always nudged him first, and when that didn't work, she pinched him. He let Roxie doze. The Reverend Nancy Keaton was admonishing the parishioners to stand with the disenfranchised, the marginalized, because, she said, Christianity is "about love."

He thought that maybe some Jews, Muslims, and even atheists might take issue with her there, since they might feel that they were "about love," too. She said they should be more supportive of the rights of their gay and lesbian, transgendered and bi-sexual brothers and sisters. He wondered if that group was singled out because Reverend Keaton had a lesbian lover—but then he felt his mother pinch him for his irreverence.

Michelle, sitting on his right, was wearing her attentive-thoughtful face, but he knew she was even more distracted than usual—probably thinking about Jake's art teacher's comments. Jake told them when he came home Friday night that his art teacher thought he had "real talent."

Jake was sitting on Michelle's right. His mouth went downwards and his neck stretched—he was suppressing a yawn. His hair, straight and very thick, was the wet straw color of Michelle's hair when she didn't have it enhanced, a kind of medium-brown underneath with shiny blond highlights. He wore it in a modified choir-boy style over the tops of his ears. For one who looked blond at first glance, he had a dark beard—Max still had a hard time thinking of Jake shaving—and surprisingly, it was thick enough to make a shadow on his cheeks if he hadn't shaved in the last twenty-four hours. Like Paul.

Like Paul. Again. There had not been an hour he hadn't thought of him since he saw him Friday evening. It seemed that all his thoughts eventually came back to Paul somehow—like now, just looking at the shadow on his son's cheek, he'd thought of Paul again. He hadn't been surprised to find himself still thinking of him on Saturday morning, but now? Now, on Sunday morning, Paul was still in the foreground of all Max's thoughts, so he had to think, or speak, *around* him, even when he was interacting with Michelle or the kids.

But it wasn't so much the fact that Max thought about him; it was the *way* he thought about him. At first he didn't notice that thinking about Paul was pleasant. When he did notice, he had to think about *why* it was pleasant. But he wasn't ready to go so far as to ask that question, so he asked himself how it was pleasant. The answer was—in the same way that thinking about dinner was pleasant when he was hungry—or, more accurately maybe, the way dinner smelled —especially something good, like steak—when he was hungry. But that was pleasant only because of the anticipation of having dinner; there was no anticipation in thinking about Paul, or was there? Yes, there was. There was the anticipation of seeing him again. That brought him back to why instead of how, so he stopped questioning himself.

Michelle leaned over and whispered, "Where are we going for lunch?"

He whispered back, "How about the Back Porch?" and she nodded. It was one of Jake's favorites.

* * *

Roxie was happily consuming great mouthfuls of her favorite item on the menu, chicken and dumplings; Jake had the house specialty, the Back Porch Burger; Max and Michelle both ordered the meatloaf, covered in mashed potatoes, cooked southern style with mayonnaise, and browned in the oven. The restaurant was crowded and noisy, popular with the Sunday after-church crowd because of its kid-friendly menu and southern cooking.

"Can I get you folks anything else?" asked the waitress. Mouths full, Michelle and Max shook their heads. She handed Max the check. "Okay, then. Y'all have a nice day now." They nodded their thanks.

"What was that art teacher's name again, Jake?" Max asked.

"Hathaway. Roscoe Hathaway. I wouldn't make too much of what he says," Jake replied, with the self-deprecating smile of one who was making very much of what the teacher had said.

Max drank down the last of the tall glass of sweet iced tea and started fumbling with the check, getting out his wallet.

"So, well—what? Is he saying that you should take art courses in college, maybe think about making it your major?" He was trying to focus his attention on a matter which he knew was very important to his son, but in the back of his mind, he thought that Jake's declared "talent" might be a reason for seeing Paul more, to show him Jake's drawings, discuss it with him. After the business about his grandmother was concluded, there would be no further excuse.

"No, Dad, he didn't have any reason for saying that I had talent. He just said it." Jake's tone showed that he was irritated by the question; it somehow diminished the significance of the compliment.

"Oh. Well—that's important, anyway." Max replied, hoping to somehow restore the significance of the teacher's remark. He was craving a cigarette. The craving was always especially strong after a meal. He turned to Michelle, "I'm going to the men's room—back in a minute."

She looked at him with half-hooded eyes and a sour expression; she knew he was going to the parking lot, and why. "Give me the check," she said. "We'll meet you at the car."

He knew he had to hurry. He threaded his way through

tables of diners, got outside to the parking lot, beeped the
Lexus open, rummaged in the glove compartment for a
smoke and a light, walked thirty feet or more away from the
car and lit up. He inhaled deeply with profound
appreciation, keeping his eye on the entrance to the
restaurant for Michelle and the kids. He didn't know why,
but Michelle's disapproval of his smoking only made him
want a cigarette all the more. It even made cigarettes taste
better. Why was that? Adolescent rebelliousness? Or was it
part of the nature of addiction?

Max puffed away too rapidly, so that the nicotine made
him dizzy—he hadn't had a cigarette since yesterday. Why
didn't the nicotine make him dizzy whenever he smoked
instead of just when he hadn't smoked in several hours? It
really was an addiction—an addiction to a drug. A friend who
was a recovering alcoholic once told him that, for an
alcoholic, there isn't enough alcohol in the world, because
the nature of alcohol addiction is that however much he
drank, he wanted more. In fact, he said, the degree of
craving is proportionate to the amount he drank. The more
he drank, the more he craved. Drinking did not satisfy a
craving—it *created* it.

Max thought now as he inhaled the dizzying smoke that
addiction was like being in love. Being near the object of
infatuation only made you want to be nearer still. For one in
love, there was not enough of the beloved's presence.
Anticipation may be the smell of a steak on the grill when a
man is hungry, but once dinner is over, that hunger is
satisfied. He knew in that moment that he wasn't anticipating
seeing Paul again—he *craved* it. And he knew very well that
once he saw him, he would only crave more....

Just then, he saw Michelle and the kids coming out of the
entrance to the restaurant. He dropped the cigarette to the
asphalt at his feet, popped a mint in his mouth, and headed
back to the car.

* * *

Jake left that afternoon at 3:00 to go back to Highland, and Roxie had gone riding at Moorhead Stables with some of her friends, not to return until about seven, in time for dinner. Max and Michelle were in the family room, reading the Sunday newspaper, when Michelle brought up a subject they'd discussed before: should Jake get a car for his sixteenth birthday?

"No," said Max.

"But think about it. If he had his own car, he wouldn't have to depend on getting a ride home with some friend or other who lives in Atlanta. He could come home whenever he felt like it."

"Yes, but now you think about it. Is it really a good idea for him to be able to come home whenever he wants to? And—and this is much more important—I know he drives well, but do you really want him driving alone on I-75 all the time? Think, Michelle."

"Well, I hadn't thought about that." She was quiet for a while. "But you know he's expecting a car, Max. All his friends get cars for their sixteenth birthdays. He'd be so disappointed. I've got an idea: suppose we get him a car, but he is to leave it at home, not take it to Highland, and he could drive it when he came home. Come to think about it, this might encourage more trips home, too."

"That's a possibility. Let me think about it for a while," he said.

They went back to reading the paper. Except for the occasional rustle of newspaper, the room was quiet for a long while. Then Michelle brought up the subject of Paul, what Max would recommend in his financial arrangements for his grandmother.

"Well, the first item of business is a will, of course, but he'll need a trustee in case his own death precedes his grandmother's. That's unlikely, of course, but he still needs to appoint somebody."

"Can you take that on?" she asked.

"Sure—because it's so unlikely, just a legal formality, really. But he might have someone else in mind—I haven't asked him." Then, as though the idea had just occurred to him, he added, "I guess I could do that now. Call him and find out, I mean. Then I could get that much done tomorrow morning and get it ready for his signature. I'll call him."

He put the paper aside and rose to go to the telephone in his study, leaving Michelle to wonder why he hadn't just used his cell phone, which was lying on the coffee table right in front of him.

CHAPTER TEN

Paul watched the sun rise over the Atlanta skyline. He loved cities—all cities. Wordworth's description of London as "that mighty heart" came to mind. There were times when he felt his aloneness more than others, but never at moments like this one, sitting on the little balcony of his apartment, sipping coffee, waiting for the day to begin, and watching the city come to life. It was odd, he thought, how being separated from the world up there twelve stories above ground made him feel so much more a part of it than when he was actually down in the city interacting with people.

At thirty-five, single, with no family to speak of, he should have been lonelier than he actually was. He'd thought about his permanently single state in the last few years. He knew several gay men who formed committed partnerships; some of them had marriage ceremonies performed, and some had adopted children, or even gone the route of artificial insemination of surrogate mothers—all to escape the fate built into an accepted gay lifestyle, the fate of having no family. Humanity is a tribal species, he thought; it was natural to desire a family. But privately—he never expressed this opinion to his gay friends—he thought that the insistence on having a family was really a rejection of one's homosexuality. It was a human phenomenon, not unique to homosexuals, as though we're all given half a glass of water, and envy makes some people see only the empty half. Married straight people sometimes envied the sexual freedom of unmarried people and created "open marriage" for themselves. People, he thought, just don't want to accept the fact that we can't have everything. The very act of choosing one thing means not choosing another thing and, like spoiled children, we throw tantrums when we can't have it all.

But maybe he could say that only because he didn't want children. He didn't know why he didn't desire a family. He certainly didn't hold the heterosexual world accountable for his aloneness, as so many angry activists did. Once, in a gay bar in San Francisco, he'd listened to some guy ranting about prejudice, discrimination and bigotry, in such foul and hateful language that he lost all patience and said, "Look, it's not straight people's fault that you're not straight," walked off and left the guy there to suffer his own invective. That was when he was in his early twenties; he didn't go to gay bars anymore. At their best—the worst was beyond thinking about—the atmosphere of manufactured cheer was depressing.

What do I have, he thought, *instead of family?* The gallery immediately came to mind, and with it, the peach coral sky floating above a blue-gray mist below, from which low, muted traffic noises were rising, announcing, *Life is waking.* He stopped thinking about what he had or didn't have—he had everything he really wanted.

He went inside to toast an English muffin, thinking about the day ahead; an appointment with a buyer for a painting priced at fifteen thousand, an interview by the arts reporter from the *Atlanta Constitution* after lunch, the call he had to make to Nana's doctor to set things in motion for the assisted living facility—which one? Who to contact?

And Max. He had called yesterday evening from his home to tell Paul he was having the will drawn up today and needed him to review and sign it. Just his voice—the low pitch and tone of it—told Paul that the suggested meeting had nothing to do with the will. This was it. It would be today, this evening, after work, at the gallery, where they were to meet at six. He knew it, and he knew this was really why he'd been sitting out there on the balcony thinking of families—an abstraction of Max's very real family.

The purpose of the call had nothing to do with the will, which could be taken care of anytime, even in the remote future. The other legal items they'd talked about were more urgent, but they would take more time to execute and Max hadn't wanted to wait. That the will was an excuse to meet right away was obvious to them both. That much was understood, though unspoken. Whether Max thought about the less-obvious meaning of the call, Paul didn't know, but he thought about it himself—very intensely if very briefly: Max had handed Paul the reins. Paul could have put off the meeting; he could even have pointed out the obvious—the will wasn't necessary, the financial plans were much more urgent, they should be arranged first, by phone mostly, and they could put off any meeting until those plans were ready. But he didn't. He suggested meeting at the gallery after closing. Paul had accepted the reins, the position of making the decision for them both.

And he was putting it off. Even thinking about the day's agenda was a way of avoiding the decision. Sometime today he must decide. He was more than a little resentful about that fact, yet he knew that Max was not capable of it, that he was confused. Whatever feelings or fantasies he may or may not have had in the past, he'd never crossed that line before.

Paul suddenly threw the muffin in the trash and walked briskly into the bedroom to dress—angry, horrified to see himself in the role of Father Murphy. But no, he thought, more calmly, as he pulled a silk tee shirt over his head—no. He had been repelled by the clumsy old priest. To this day, he didn't know why he had submitted to him. No—no, that wasn't true. He knew why. He had simply decided it was time to lose his virginity, and the priest gave him the perfect safe opportunity to do so. Father Murphy was completely non-dangerous—emotionally, socially—in every way. That the stupid man believed himself responsible for the incident only increased Paul's repugnance.

That was not the case with Max. Max was in love. Paul knew that. It didn't occur to him then to ask himself whether he was, too. The urgency of the decision he had to make overrode such an extraneous consideration.

All day it stayed in front of him, like a lens through which he saw everything else—the buyer, the reporter, and the thousand little details of the day. Yet, even at four o'clock, when he called down to the security guard to tell him that Max would be arriving after the gallery was closed, he still had not decided.

He knew that no decision was itself a decision. He remembered a friend he'd had in Savannah years ago named Pamela, whom he had taken to an abortion clinic.

"Good grief, Pam, what do you have against birth control?" It was the second time he'd taken her on that dismal errand. They were driving to the clinic in his old Thunderbird.

"Well, I don't know. I guess because I want it to be—spontaneous, you know? I don't want making love to be some kind of decision; I want it to be something that just happens."

"But that's not realistic, is it? That's not honest." They were silent for a moment; then, in rising resentment, he blurted out: "What do you think sex is for anyway, Pam?" That angered her, and she turned in the passenger seat and said pointedly, "Well, gee, Paul. I guess I don't know, do I. Suppose you tell me what it's for." Point taken, he'd thought, and apologized.

But here he was, knowing well that making no decision was a decision. Somehow he couldn't do it. He couldn't picture it. He didn't want to be the predator he felt that he was, given Max's naiveté. And above all, he thought of Michelle, Roxanne, and the son he hadn't yet met. It was wrong, wrong, wrong.

Then it was six o'clock and the in-house phone rang.

"Mr. Meyer, Mr. Maxwell's here; I've sent him on up."

"Okay. Thanks."

And then there he was, coming through the glass door of Paul's office. "Hi," Max said. He didn't even have the will with him. All pretenses were gone. But there was still time—put it off, *delay, delay.*

"Hi," Paul answered, his throat constricted. "Hey, how long's it been since you had a tour of the gallery?" *Delay, delay.* But he already knew he was taking Max home, and Max knew it, too.

"Quite a while, really. Since before you came."

Paul went around the desk and threw his arm around Max's shoulders, even though that was difficult, given Max's height and the breadth of his shoulders, but it was casual, it was such a "just-buddies" gesture—*there was still time. It wasn't too late.*

"Well, I'll just show you a couple of the highlights, new stuff since you were here, on the way down to the garage." That was it. He'd admitted they were leaving—and leaving together.

Max dutifully walked around wherever Paul led him, reading titles of the works, until Paul said, teasingly, "Hey, don't read titles. This is art, not literature."

The tour didn't last long. Art held no interest for either of them. In an almost drunken playfulness, they turned the corner on the mezzanine and Max stopped, arrested by the giant canvas on the facing wall. "My God," he said slowly.

"Yeah, that's the Mayfield. He's a new artist from the Midwest—Kansas, I think. Probably where he got that light."

The painting was about ten square feet of stunning outward ray-like strokes. Max walked closer to read the title: *Coeur de Lion.* "Heart of the Lion," he read aloud. "Wow."

"It's the only one we have at the moment. He's still pretty much unknown, but he's got an exhibit coming up in three months at the High. It's not for sale now because the price will probably double after the exhibit."

Max walked backwards across the room to get the view the painting demanded. "I know you said it doesn't matter what the titles are. We're looking at art, not reading literature, and all that. But why *heart* of the lion? There's no heart—I mean, I don't know how he did it, but all this outward motion comes from a center that isn't there."

Paul cocked his head to the side a little. "I see what you mean." Then he grinned mischievously. "But leave it to a lawyer to point that out," he laughed softly, a laugh that sounded to Max like audible silk. "You've got to argue, don't you, just can't help it—always looking for evidence, for proof of something." He shook his finger at Max in mock chastisement. Max took the finger between his own, as though he were picking a ripe strawberry, and then reached beyond it for Paul's hand.

They laughed together then, out loud, and the moment turned into childlike, affectionate play, as a blanket descended from somewhere and wrapped around them, close and intimate. Max glanced sideways, almost shyly, at Paul's laughing profile. His lip, over his perfect white teeth, its finely chiseled, almost feminine bow—just that, just the bow of Paul's lip, flooded him with warmth, with *joy.* Max could not remember when he'd been this happy. He had the sensation that this moment was all that could ever be hoped for, longed for. He felt, in fact, that passionate conviction reserved for lovers: This moment was the meaning of his life.

PART II

JUNE

CHAPTER ELEVEN

Michelle sat at her computer updating IRS information for the Hunter Gallery. As a non-profit foundation, the gallery was exempt from most—but not all—federal tax; however, the maintenance procedure for that status was complicated, very involved, and not something she could manage to do with only half her attention. Local and state taxes required even more attention to detail, and she'd have to update those files after she finished the federal pages.

It was no good. She wasn't paying attention to the tax programs. She might as well pause and think through the news flash Roxie had given her this morning: Puberty had arrived during the night. There had been no chance for Roxie to tell her at breakfast; the news had to wait until they were in the car on the way to St. Joseph's Academy. That meant a stop on the way at a drugstore for necessary supplies, but it also meant they couldn't talk then. Michelle would have to wait until this evening for the mother-daughter conversation that would be a hallmark in both their lives.

Her feelings were completely mixed; worse, they were tangled up with thoughts. Michelle was a practical woman, very smart about some things that people who didn't know her well would not have credited her with. People who knew her only slightly thought of her as rather unemotional, though not unkind. They may have thought that apart from being intelligent and an excellent manager, her most admirable trait was that she was beautiful without being vain. But Michelle possessed another quality unsuspected by most people. She wasn't just smart—she was wise.

This moment was an example of that wisdom. She knew her first task was to separate the practical thoughts from the mixed feelings and decided she would deal with the thoughts first. Thoughts were always easier than feelings; they were intelligible, but feelings were not as easily identified, often open-ended, and even unintelligible. First—a visit to the doctor to make sure all was well. Roxie had never had a pelvic exam, had never been to a gynecologist before. She'd call her pediatrician, tell him the news and ask his advice about this. If the exam wasn't advised, she certainly didn't want to put Roxie through it.

She thought she should also contact Roxie's gym teacher, find out what her policy was for students when they were having their period. Probably there was no policy at all these days; teachers treated children now in ways that seemed purposely to disregard gender distinctions. But if genetics played a role here, Roxie would have a hard time, and she'd need exemption from some gym activities. Until Jake was born, Michelle had always had difficult periods.

Then she thought a more practical procedure would be to call the school nurse instead of the gym teacher. And finally, as though she were checking off items on a list, she knew without thinking about it that Roxie didn't need any education about what was happening to her; that wasn't a problem, but there would be other information needed, and advice about the practical side of things. They could talk about that this evening. School would be out at the end of the week. The timing was good: Roxie would have the summer to get used to the changes in her body and in her life.

Okay, now for the feelings. Tears came. They surprised her a bit. Her little girl was no longer her little girl. She allowed her feelings to surface and articulate themselves. This moment, this time of change in her child's life was also a change in her own. And it marked a change in their relationship. It wasn't to her father that Roxie delivered her news this morning, but to her mother. More tears came. Roxie was no longer just the child of her parents. Now, she was, in a new way, her mother's daughter. There was an enclosure there, just the two of them together, a new friendship, an intimacy based on their shared femininity. She was stunned for a moment by the fact, the evidential fact, that Roxie herself had intuited that change, when she chose to tell her mother in private, and not to include her father in the news, knowing—Michelle felt certain of this—that it was her mother's place to inform her father, not hers. There was a place now where her daddy, beloved though he was, was not invited. Max would have to deal with that change, too.

And meanwhile, both of them together—she and Max—would mark this day as the beginning of a long slow loss that would culminate only many years hence, when their little Roxanne became someone's wife, someone's mother. Should she call him now, tell him the news? No, she'd wait till tonight when they were alone, after she'd had the conversation with Roxie that had to happen first.

She buzzed Lolly, the secretary she shared with Paul, and told her she didn't want to be disturbed for any reason. She even locked her office door and pushed the button on her phone to turn the ringer off. The occasion was somewhat momentous. She needed to feel, to think, to—pray. But she couldn't pray; she didn't know how. All she could do was to whisper, "If you're there, look after my baby, please. Keep her from all hurt...."

* * *

Paul had completed his research into assisted living facilities in the Atlanta area. He eliminated most of them by checking a list of criteria he'd put together for that purpose. Private nurses or nursing assistants? Access to doctors, specialists? Access to clergy and religious services—what kind? The apartments, space, floorplans, amenities. Is physical therapy available? What sort of social activities are provided? He found that most places had very flexible arrangements, designed for the differing needs of patients—

who were called "residents"—but one thing was common to all of them: they were expensive. In fact, Dr. Hernandez's estimate of 7,000 dollars per month turned out to be conservative. Likely, he'd had Savannah facilities in mind; in Atlanta, everything cost more.

And that was another issue. He hadn't told Nana yet that he wanted to move her to Atlanta. Savannah was just too far away for him to keep an eye on things. Besides, it looked as though he'd be selling the gallery in Savannah now, anyway. He had checked into taking out another mortgage on it, but when he told his manager Peg Litchfield, she said she wanted to buy it herself. She and her husband were discussing it. They said they would make him an offer the next time he returned.

Everything was moving along, but nothing was firm yet. Max had been advising him all the way. Last night, he'd told Paul that he should do nothing else until he told Nana his plans and got her approval and consent. He had come to rely heavily on Max for this kind of advice—and for so much else. In fact, his life, since Max came into it, had utterly changed. Nothing would ever be the same again—because *he* would never be the same.

He was cooking now, trying a recipe he'd gotten from DeJong's, a restaurant he and Max tried out last week. Max had raved about the cheese and crab dish there, so Paul got the recipe from the chef. If he could replicate it, he'd cook it for Max.

DeJong's was frequented by a disproportionate number of Atlanta's gay community. Paul wasn't sure why, maybe because the owner was a prominent member of that community, but there was also something about the décor, the ambiance—somehow it simply appealed to gay people, especially gay men of the upper class, and those who aspired to that class. In fact, Paul had muddled the question around a bit when he was there with Max and decided that the appeal was *taste*. Everything about the restaurant—the menu, the wine list, the expensive antique furniture, the shaded blue-gray walls—everything was in such excellent taste. DeJong's did not advertise, yet reservations sometimes had to be booked weeks in advance. There was something in gay men, including himself, that made them gravitate toward refinements in taste. Max had declared it the best restaurant he'd ever visited, and Paul had basked in that intense gratification he'd come to feel every time he thought he had pleased Max in some way.

There was some concern about going out in public that way, but if there was any place where discretion could be taken for granted, DeJong's was that place. Max had even recognized a couple of people there—much to his surprise, in pairs of two men—and Paul was amused by his reaction. In so many ways, Max was like a kid exploring a whole new world, and a whole side of himself that he never knew existed. If Paul had any lingering concern about being a Father Murphy figure in Max's life, it was over now. Max was gay. He just hadn't known it before.

Paul was happy—so happy that he believed he'd never really been happy before in his whole life. He smiled, drizzling the sherry into the cheese sauce, remembering how he'd sat on his balcony only two months ago and believed himself content with his lack of connection with others, lack of family, lack of real intimacy. But how could he have known then what he was missing?

He dipped his finger into the sauce and put it to his lips, almost like a kiss. It was delicious. Everything tasted better now, looked better, sounded better—*life* was better. With effort, he turned his thoughts again to Nana. He was going to Savannah tomorrow to talk everything over with her. He had narrowed down his list of facilities to three, and he was taking brochures for her to study, but he knew the big issue would not be the facility but the location. And he had never responded to her plaintive desire to go "home" to Spain. That was out of the question, but he was going to suggest a trip to Barcelona when he saw her tomorrow to talk about the move. Max had said he thought that would probably be enough for her, and Paul was sure he was right, sure that Nana had no idea how much things had changed in Spain since the last time she was there. It had to be more than thirty years ago, and she had no family there now. A short trip would open her eyes to the reality of Barcelona now; she'd see for herself that it was not the city of her childhood memories.

He turned his attention back to the cheese sauce, stirring it slowly and constantly, just as DeJong's chef had instructed. He had even bought an expensive copper double-boiler for that purpose, just because the chef had recommended it. If the dish turned out right, he would surprise Max with it when he got back from Savannah.

CHAPTER TWELVE

Max's reaction to Michelle's news surprised her. She had expected him to be somewhat wistful, a little sentimental, maybe; she had not expected him to be emotional. Max wasn't an emotional man in the first place, and this news, while it marked the end of Roxie's childhood—physiologically, anyway—was not a cause for tears. But he actually had tears in his eyes when she told him that Roxie had started her periods.

Max was different lately in other ways. He seemed to be emotional about things he scarcely noticed in the past. Jake was coming home for the summer on Friday, and Max had been as jubilant as Roxie when they talked about it at dinner. And in the kitchen after dinner, he'd been excited about the prospect of telling Jake he'd get a car for his birthday.

"Max, you're not going to tell him *now*, are you? His birthday's not until September."

"No, of course not. But I can hardly wait. He'll be so happy. We haven't talked about what kind of car, you know. What do you think? It should be something he can feel proud of."

"Yes, but remember the deal. He's not to drive it on the interstate or to take it back to Highland with him. It has to stay here, so I don't think any kind of super-powered car is appropriate. How about a Honda Civic? A Nissan, maybe?"

"Oh, come on, Michelle. He has to have something to show off to his friends—something a little sexier than a Civic, don't you think?"

"No, Max, I don't think. Eddie Ferguson's parents bought him a Civic."

"Yeah, well, that's the Fergusons." He paused, then said

in a way that Michelle thought would mean a bit of an argument, "We can talk about it later. There's plenty of time to decide."

She was afraid he was going to push for something he called "sexier;" she certainly hoped he didn't have some kind of sports car in mind—that would be dangerous. But what concerned Michelle almost as much was the change in Max. When they first talked about it, he'd had to be convinced that Jake should have a car at all; now he wanted him to have something flashy, and possibly dangerous. And those tears over Roxie's entrance into puberty. Lately, Max seemed a little—*childish*. A couple of times a week now he went riding with Roxie—or he played water polo with her and her friends in the pool. Now, he was talking about taking Jake on a fishing trip to Alaska with Paul. There was certainly nothing wrong with any of this, and part of her was happy to see him less serious than he usually was. It was just that it was so unlike him. She had begun to feel a little lonely in her parenting role, a little burdened by her own adulthood.

She lay in bed that night thinking about this change, unnoticeable, probably, to anyone else. Lying on her back, looking up at the ceiling, and feeling lonely for the first time in her marriage, she thought about another difference: Sex was less frequent—that did not concern her much—but there was something else. Always in the past, no matter which of them initiated love-making, neither of them had ever rejected the other, never made excuses, never showed a lack of responsiveness. Tonight, Max had made a little reflexive movement of his shoulder away from her when she touched his neck with her fingers. It was the first time she had experienced what she knew to be rejection.

* * *

"Okay," Paul said into the speaker of his cell phone while he drove up the ramp to get on Interstate 16, "I'm going to talk to her today about a short vacation trip to Barcelona—maybe a week, or even a little less. Wish me luck."

"I do," Max answered. "I honestly think that when she sees how the city has changed, she won't even recognize it. She certainly won't think of it as 'home' anymore—with no family left there, especially. You're her family now. You're all she has. And that fact, by the way, is what will make it less difficult for her to make the move to Atlanta. You're here—and she'll want to be wherever you are."

"God, I hope you're right. You usually are. By the way, find some way to have dinner when I get back tomorrow, okay? I've got a surprise for you."

Max smiled. It was partly a smile of anticipation but mostly one of tenderness, a feeling he always had when he sensed Paul's endearing, childlike desire to please him. "Now, what are you planning?" he asked, in the teasing tone of the banter-like communication that had become habitual between them.

"Ha. Not going to tell you. Wait and see. Think you can manage it?"

Max sobered. "No. Jake's due home. Remember?"

"Oh, yes, I forgot. That's okay. How about Sunday night?"

"That should be workable. I'll call you."

It took no effort on Paul's part to avoid expressing disappointment, regardless of the twinge it inevitably caused him. Max's family came first. Indeed, if it were possible, Max's family was more important to Paul than to Max himself. Every tiny bit of news, every little incident with the children—though never with Michelle—was a matter of great interest, great importance to Paul. He delighted in the little reports of Roxie's childish remarks or escapades, of Jake's timid conviction that he had artistic talent while pretending it didn't matter—so typically macho for a teen-aged boy. Sometimes, he felt that he was a part of the family—and once or twice, he even felt that Max's children were his own.

Talking about the children was easy, natural. Michelle's absence from their conversation was conspicuous, a fact they had not discussed, but one that constantly worried Paul. What was he to do with her? What were they to do with her? The subject had to be addressed. He did not know what Max felt, what he thought. He knew what *he* felt—a sincere love for Michelle, a great respect, and even a kind of protective loyalty. He could not bear the thought of Michelle being hurt in any way by anybody—including Max. There was no way he would ever allow that to happen.

CHAPTER THIRTEEN

Jake was cooking hamburgers on the grill by the pool. He and Max had competed last year in a burger cook-off and he'd won by the unanimous vote of twelve people. It had been his job ever since, but fortunately, he enjoyed it. Michelle sat at a table, sipping a glass of wine as she watched her son turning the hamburgers, giving orders to Roxie, and even to Max, about making the salad, and setting the table. He was as tall as his father—over six feet already and still growing. She thought he might even end up taller than Max, who was six feet and two inches. She wondered if he would eventually be as big, also, and possibly develop high blood pressure, as Max had done—just like his father before him. It had been that unchecked blood pressure that killed Max's father. She knew his not-so-secret smoking habit wasn't helping his blood pressure; it made her angry with him just to think about it.

But it was Jake who was on her mind now. He'd inherited the Maxwell physique but his coloring came from her side of the family—dark blond with blue eyes. At this stage of his development, he was a strikingly handsome boy and she felt a little burst of maternal pride in him. More important, though, was the way he was developing intellectually—and artistically. He'd brought a letter home with him from his art teacher at Highland, and Michelle was impressed enough by the teacher's obvious knowledge of art to believe the letter was sincere in its praise of Jake's talent. It was time to take this matter seriously. She decided that she would ask to see his sketchbook after dinner.

Max was horsing around with Roxie, throwing her back into the pool every time she climbed out. He didn't look any

slimmer despite the work-outs he'd started at a gym near his
office. He had been going to the gym for two hours or so at
least three times a week. She thought the work-outs should
have had more visible effect by now. On Friday he
announced that he would go on Sunday evening as well.

"Jake, when will the burgers be ready?" she asked.

"In about two minutes. You guys need to dry off and sit
down," he yelled at Max and Roxie. "Mom, you can dress
the salad."

"Okay." She rose and went to the work counter by the
grill, stirred the blue cheese dressing—Jake's favorite—and
dressed the salad. "Listen, Jake. I want to look at your
sketchbook. That letter from Mr. Hathaway is impressive—
no, really, it is. I haven't seen any of your sketches in a whole
year. Why haven't you brought them home?"

"Well, I guess because there are other things I want to do
when I come home. I only brought one sketchbook with
me."

Michelle raised her sunglasses to rest on top of her head
and looked at him. "How many do you have?" she asked.

"Maybe half a dozen or so."

"Really? That many?"

"Yeah. Pass me the plates, please." They were silent then,
Michelle thinking about the fact that Jake had filled six
sketchbooks. He wasn't drawing for class assignments only—
he was forming a work habit. The last time she'd seen his
work she'd been impressed by his sensitivity to shadow. He'd
drawn trees, faces, and rather odd stills, mostly in pencil, but
he was beginning to experiment with charcoal and pastels.
She carried the salad and bowls to the table, then helped him
carry plates of hamburgers and grilled buns. Max and Roxie
sat waiting with towels wrapped around their waists and
shoulders. Why hadn't he brought all the sketchbooks
home? She realized with a little start that he'd lost the
childish desire to "show off" his drawings. He was taking a
proprietary attitude toward them now, the way an artist might

do when a bond formed between himself and his work.

"Well, I want to see your sketchbook as soon as we've finished eating, okay?"

He seemed a little hesitant, not answering right away. "Okay, but it's not much."

* * *

Paul wondered if this obstinacy was part of Nana's encroaching dementia. She'd never been so assertive before.

"Paul, I'm not moving to Atlanta. I don't like Atlanta. Yes, of course, I want to be near you—but, you know, dear, this job you have now may not last forever. You'll come back to your gallery here."

"Nana, I just told you, I'm selling the gallery."

"But why?"

"Because, darling, I need the revenue to finance assisted living for you."

"But you wouldn't have to do that if I didn't move into that place in Atlanta. Paul, I'm not going. You tell Peg you're not selling the gallery. I'm staying right here."

Paul's hands were clasped, hanging down between his knees as he sat on the sofa, leaning earnestly toward her in the living room of her condo. It wasn't going well. She leaned back in her chair, away from him.

"Listen, dear," he said patiently. "Dr. Hernandez says that the dementia will progress. You can't live alone anymore, Nana." Why was she being unreasonable? Was it part of the disease?

"I know that. I'm not completely batty—not yet. I know I'm going to need somebody to stay with me. But there are other solutions. I hate Atlanta. It's not a place anyone should have to live if they don't need to be there for work. You do— I don't. And you don't really have to, either. You could come back to Savannah and take care of your own gallery, not someone else's."

He had to admit that she was right. And it dawned on him for the first time that his choice of solutions had risen out of his own rather selfish consideration of what was good for his career. He hadn't even considered returning to Savannah—giving up his position at Hunter. He would also have to give up the offer to write an art column for the *Atlanta Constitution*, if he returned. It would mean reversing the upward movement of his career.

"This place is big enough for both of us, Paul—unless you want the privacy of living alone. If you do, that's fine, you could live somewhere else. I could have day care when the time comes—or if you want to live somewhere else, I could have a live-in. It would still be cheaper than moving to Atlanta—and you wouldn't have to go into debt."

He leaned back now on the sofa. He was finding it hard to argue with the common sense solution that he hadn't even considered. He realized that he'd been blinded to it by his own ambition. He sighed. "I just want you near me, Nana," he said.

But he also knew there was another reason now that he could not leave Atlanta—Max. Leaving Atlanta was out of the question, even if he'd been willing to sacrifice his career. And he couldn't tell her about that. It was that part of his life that had always been closed to her—and always would be.

She smiled. "My darling boy. You're thirty-five years old now. Don't you think you're grown up enough to leave your Nana?"

He tried to look a little hurt, though he was ashamed of the ploy. "I guess I thought you'd want to be near me."

She laughed a little, letting him know that she was aware of the ploy. "Well, dear, if you're not grown up enough—I am." Then she narrowed her eyes a little. "You know very well what *I* want."

"Nana, you have no idea what Spain is like now. And you have no one there. But that's something else I wanted to talk to you about anyway." He brightened, glad to be able to say something he knew would please her. "Let's take a little trip to Barcelona next month, okay? Think you'd like a little vacation with me?"

But again, she was ahead of him. "I know you're thinking that I wouldn't like what I'd find. I know that Spain is now in the European Union, and not the strong and independent Catholic country it was when I was a girl. It was still under Franco then. I've been keeping up with the news, dear. I know what it's like now—at least, insofar as I *can* know without actually being there. And you're wrong. I have nieces and nephews there. Even though I've never met them, they are there. And they are my family."

"They wouldn't look after you, darling. They don't even know you."

"And they won't—unless I go to meet them."

* * *

The trip had not been a success, and Paul drove back to Atlanta that night feeling depressed. He didn't listen to music as he usually did on the long drive, didn't call Michelle at the gallery—or Max—and he didn't think about the coming week's agenda. He thought about nothing except Nana's obstinacy. It made him angry, hurt, confused. He'd never felt so out of control, nor so vaguely, unaccountably, guilty.

It was Max who'd made him think about Nana's wishes in the first place. Maybe he never should have asked her what she wanted, maybe he should have just taken over and done what he thought was right. That was what he'd always done. He had the feeling that he'd opened a door now that would not close again. Worse, he was also aware that the door had opened a moral question that he couldn't quite formulate. He struggled now to let that question go, knowing instinctively that once it was actually articulated, he'd have to answer it, and he didn't want to.

And while he drove, he thought from time to time that, at least he'd see Max tomorrow, cook for him, just be with him

—he didn't even want to make love—just be with him. Being with Max always made him feel secure, strong—as though all was as it should be, as it should have always been. A cold hard knot formed then, like a physical stone lodged in his chest: as it "should be" was not the way it was, it was not reality. Reality was a big three-story brick house, where a family lived, where children slept and a grandmother visited, where people gathered at a table, in laughter and light. And where was he? He was alone, in shadows on a dark and lonely road in the middle of nowhere. The brick house passed from his thoughts, but the cold knot remained. He knew it was fear—fear of losing Max. He'd never been vulnerable before, never let his happiness depend on someone else.

He felt so helpless. Like a child, dependent on the mercy and wisdom of the adults around him who seemed to have charge of him, to have control of his fate. There had to have been a time, a time he didn't remember, when he'd been in that position before, the position of helpless, frightened vulnerability—otherwise, how could he have recognized it? How could it have the power to generate such fear in him now?

The sparse traffic in the flat rural Georgia landscape, the blackness of the night, broken only by the high, remote, impersonal overhead lights of the interstate threatened to swallow him. He glanced at the speedometer—he was doing eighty-five, but he felt stuck in the thick blackness. Finally, traffic picked up—and lights—as he approached the Piedmont south of the sprawling Atlanta suburbs. The city awaited him —and civilization—away from the wild power of unpredictable and primitive nature. He switched on the jazz channel of his satellite radio. His apartment, his haven above the lights of the city waited for him—and Max. Max would be there tomorrow.

CHAPTER FOURTEEN

Max was genuinely surprised to hear about the reaction of Paul's grandmother to his plans to move her closer to him. From everything Paul had told him, his "Nana" was devoted to him. Maybe he had mistaken Paul's devotion for hers. His instinctive defensiveness of Paul made him begin to question this unknown elderly woman's love for her grandson. While the questioning couldn't be called suspicion, exactly, it did lay the groundwork for a belief that he, Max, held Paul's interests closer to heart than this beloved grandmother did.

When Paul had talked about his Nana in the past, his obvious love for her had caused Max to feel an affection for her—as an extension of Paul, who, more and more, became the very center of Max's life. Knowing that he himself could not bear allowing more than three days to pass without being with Paul, he could not help but wonder how this woman—regardless of how attached she might be to her condo, her friends, her church—how could she turn down an opportunity to live close to Paul? He began to understand that he, and he alone, truly loved Paul.

This conviction inspired within him a protectiveness that would have been otherwise inexplicable—even among lovers. True, erotic love was more binding than most others, but surely not more binding than the parental love that Paul *thought* he'd always had from his grandmother, the love he should have had—and did not—from his own parents, especially his father. Knowing Paul's past evoked in Max a tender and unaccustomed kind of pity, especially for his father's abandonment of him when he was a child.

But there was an inescapable question implied in Max's reflection on the deprivation Paul had suffered, and to his credit, Max did not try to avoid it: If erotic love was not as binding as parental love, did he love Paul more than he loved Roxie and Jake? Typically, Max raised questions he did not answer. Once the question was asked, he no longer considered it—as though the question itself were an answer. It never occurred to Max that asking such questions did not constitute answers; he believed—without knowing what he believed—that the formulation of a question by itself was the expression of moral conscience. This intellectual habit had been acquired unconsciously over a lifetime of adherence to an existential ethic that distrusted, even disallowed, answers. Unconscious of the habit, Max was unaware that it made it possible for him to avoid the kind of direct accountability from himself that answers provide, even as the questions he raised permitted—often demanded—that accountability from others—in this case, from Paul's grandmother.

"I don't want to hurt your feelings, Paul—God knows I don't." He put his large protective hand over Paul's smaller one with its long slender fingers, where it lay in seeming inert helplessness on the table. "But do you think—maybe—that she really doesn't care that much about being close to you? And don't you think—in that case—that maybe it shouldn't be so important to you?"

Paul winced. The question was painful, but he had come to recognize that hard truths could be expected from Max. Max asked questions he never asked of himself. In fact, it was only since knowing Max that he even recognized he'd never asked tough questions before, perhaps he'd never dared—worse, perhaps he'd never cared enough. Max was awakening in him a kind of morality that he'd never known, a toughness, an honesty, an almost manly kind of fortitude he had not possessed before—hadn't even known, until Max.

The love Paul felt for him transcended mere sexual attraction to become deeper and more profound every day. It was beautiful to Paul, so beautiful sometimes that it almost seemed he couldn't bear it. And now this simple question, about whether Nana really wanted to be near him, proved something else to Paul: Max really cared about him, really loved him. He bit his lower lip to keep tears from welling in his eyes. He felt blessed. He brought Max's hand to his lips and kissed it, unable to speak.

It was especially difficult for Max to leave then, but he had already spent more time at Paul's apartment than he intended. A trip to the gym on a Sunday, so soon after Jake had come home, could not be expected to last for more than a couple of hours.

* * *

Monday morning, Michelle held the intercom button down: "Paul, have you got a minute?"

"Sure. Come on in."

Michelle came into the office carrying a large portfolio. "I'm going to leave these here. Look at them when you have a chance, please." She stood the portfolio by the side of his desk. "We can talk about them later," she said, heading back to the door. "I'm taking off for a while. Got to take Roxie to the doctor."

"Oh? Is everything okay?"

"Oh, yeah. Just an exam. I'm sure you know these are Jake's drawings. I was reluctant to show them to you before, when I thought he'd want me to. Now when I want to, he's reluctant to let me." She smiled at the irony and breezed out of the office.

On the way down to the parking garage, she thought about the drawings, and wondered what Paul would say about them. She had spread them out on the kitchen island, careful with the onionskin tissue that protected each one. They were charcoal, and Jake had not applied any kind of fixative. He stood at the sink drinking a coke while she examined them. For a long time, she simply didn't know what to say. They were wonderful. Jake's experimentation with shadow had developed into a technique. The last was the best. It was a portrait of Roxie, drawn from memory. He'd started, so it seemed, from a page all in shadow, and Roxie's face, laughing—so like the way she looked sometimes when she was riding—seemed to emerge from the shadow as points of light. It was lovely.

"Jake, I want this, okay? I want to frame it and put it in the family room."

He blushed. "Oh, come on, Mom. You don't have to do that."

She looked up at him as if she were looking at someone else, someone not her son—an artist. "I don't think you understand, honey. This isn't your mama talking. This is somebody who knows a thing or two about art. Jake, this is wonderful—and you're only sixteen. What on earth will you produce in five years or so?" She paused. It seemed as though it was too much to take in. "Go get your daddy. I want him to see these."

"Oh, good grief, Mom."

"Go get him."

Max came in from the family room, followed by Roxie, still wet from swimming. Michelle caught her just as she reached toward the island counter.

"Uh, uh, young lady—not with wet hands. You're not supposed to come in wet anyway. You know that. Go dry off."

Roxie padded out and Max leaned over the drawings. "Oh, wow," he said, then repeated, "Wow."

"Yeah," Michelle answered. "I know." And they both looked at Jake as though he were some strange artist hiding in their son's skin.

* * *

Dr. Stratham had been recommended by Roxie's pediatrician. She was not Michelle's own gynecologist, whom she somehow distrusted with Roxie. She just couldn't imagine her own gynecologist—a man—for Roxie, so the pediatrician had recommended Dr. Stratham, who was a young woman, and Michelle felt more comfortable about that situation. The pediatrician had assured her that no exam would be necessary but agreed that it was a good idea to establish a relationship before an exam became necessary.

As it turned out, Dr. Stratham only set up a medical record for Roxie and asked her questions. Some of the questions obviously embarrassed Roxie, and Michelle was glad she hadn't taken her to a male doctor. She also asked Michelle questions about her own medical history and made some notes on Roxie's newly established record. Then she asked to talk to Michelle alone, and Roxie was sent to the waiting room to watch TV.

"I'm sure you know, Mrs. Maxwell, that children reach sexual maturity at a younger age now."

"Yes, I know. Roxie's only eleven. I didn't start having periods until I was thirteen."

"Well, this also means they become sexually active much younger now. I don't know how you and Roxie's father feel about the fact that your children may become sexually active much earlier than you did, but...." She trailed off, apparently expecting Michelle to pick up the thread.

"Dr. Stratham, are you suggesting birth control for my little girl?"

"Well, no, Mrs. Maxwell, but I think you should read some literature on the subject ahead of that time." She reached into a top drawer of her desk, withdrew several pamphlets and handed them to Michelle.

"My God," murmured Michelle. But she took the pamphlets and shoved them into her handbag. On the drive back home to drop Roxie off, she felt stunned. From time to time, she glanced at Roxie, flat-chested, whose legs barely touched the floor, who chattered about utterly childish things. Next week, her little girl would be vaccinated against a type of cervical cancer that is transmitted by a virus during sexual intercourse. "My God," she repeated.

CHAPTER FIFTEEN

"Good grief! The only 'boy' Roxie's interested in is Sampson." Michelle said to Paul when she returned to the office, still reacting to the doctor's advice to have Roxie vaccinated against viral cervical cancer.

"Sampson? Isn't that her horse?" Paul was amused by Michelle's reaction.

"Yeah—and I don't think bestiality has become socially acceptable yet."

Paul laughed out loud. "Well, I don't know. But listen, I looked at Jake's work." He became serious as he took the sketch of Roxie from the portfolio. "Michelle, what are you and Max going to do about this?"

"So you're as impressed as I am? I'm so glad to hear it. Mama judgments aren't trustworthy; that's why I wanted you to look at it. What strikes me most is the progress he's made in less than a year. I mean—a year ago, he was talented—we knew that. But his talent seemed to be in creating likenesses, you know? He'd begun to experiment a little, but mostly, he was just extraordinarily good at likeness representations. But this—" She broke off, not sure how to complete the thought.

"Let's just say it, okay?" Paul finished her thought for her. "I think we should just say it out loud. Jake is gifted. I think he's the real thing—that is, if he keeps interested, if he keeps it up. So I'm asking—what are you going to do about this?"

"Well, we're not sure. It doesn't much depend on us, really, but on him. As you said, *if* he keeps interested...I think our difficulty in this is not so much how to encourage, but maybe even *whether* we should encourage him at all."

Paul frowned and so did Michelle. They both sat in silence for a moment, considering how best to foster the talent of young Jacob Maxwell. Paul was aware that he was thinking not only as an art critic confronted with Jake as a possible new talent, but also, almost as a father, confronted with evidence that his son is gifted.

"I know what you mean," he said. "What's best for Jake?"

"Oh, I'm so glad you understand. I mean, it's thrilling to me, of course, and Max is very proud. But that's us. What does Jake want?"

Her question caused Paul to remember Max's question of him two months ago: What did she—his Nana—want? And his own sudden realization that he'd never considered what Nana wanted. He was learning so much, growing so much, as a person, a human being, since he'd begun to love Max. He had to look away for a moment, afraid of what his eyes, full of reverence for that love and for the beloved, might reveal. It happened more and more often now, this awareness that he'd never really loved before, never knew what it meant to love before. He was often overwhelmed by a feeling of *blessedness*, a conviction that he'd been blessed somehow, and a need, an actual *need*, to express gratitude. It was that need to express gratitude that was almost making him believe in God again, as though God existed because Paul needed him to—he needed him to exist so that he could thank him for Max.

Michelle was looking at the sketch of Roxie, her head tilted to the side a bit, and a gentle smile in her eyes as well as on her lips. "It almost looks as if he's sketching with light."

Paul stared at the sketch with her. "I wonder if—Michelle, did you ask him whether he's using paint at all?"

"I know what you're wondering—whether he could transfer that light to another medium. No, I didn't ask him. I'm almost as afraid to ask him questions as I am to make statements." She sighed, took the sketch from him and put it back in the portfolio. "But I've got to get over this caution. I think it's excessive, and it comes from maternalism more than it does from criticism." She gathered up the portfolio and said, "Paul, would you talk to him? He could listen to you without imputing any motivation to you. He'd believe you—you're not emotionally involved with him."

Paul felt himself make a little start, jolted back to the present reality, the issue at hand and Michelle's presence. "Of course. How do you want to arrange that?"

"Come to dinner, okay? No. I just thought of something. He said the other day that he wants to tour the gallery. Let's do it that way. Give him a tour—or *I'll* give him a tour, and then we'll have lunch with you. How's that?"

"Would Max be joining us?" He hoped not. He'd been with Max in the presence of his family a couple of times and it made him uncomfortable.

"No. Just us. I think it would be better if it were just us 'professionals,' you know?" She laughed a little.

He smiled. It was a good arrangement, a workable plan. He thought he'd be able to communicate with Jake much better if his father wasn't there.

After Michelle left his office, Paul sat thinking about Jake a few minutes. When he met him, what had impressed him first was the boy's unusual good looks, then his quiet, attentive personality. He was very good-natured, with none of the surliness that so often affected boys that age and made them such a trial to other people, especially their parents. Jake's capacity for attentiveness reminded Paul of Nana, as though he were completely extroverted, with no self-preoccupation, no self-consciousness of any kind. It was clear that he adored his little sister, and Paul thought how lucky Roxie was—how lucky they all were—to have each other. Once, when he was sitting poolside with Michelle and watching the kids cavorting in the pool, he felt like a protective spirit, hovering around this family, so precious to him, though not his own. Then Max came through the glass doors carrying a tray of drinks, and the feeling vanished.

It was not pleasant now to recall that afternoon at the Maxwell house, the first time he'd felt that discomfort when he was with the family in Max's presence. When it happened again later, he promised himself that he wouldn't get in that position again. He didn't mention it to Max; they never talked about the family collectively, just as they never talked about Michelle.

Max wasn't coming over that afternoon, or that night. It would be a good time to get some work done at the office and to make some concrete plans to take Nana to Barcelona for a couple of weeks, and he decided to follow through with a phone call to a travel agent recommended by a friend in Spain. When the international connection was made and he'd asked for Señor Rivera in English, he was told he'd have to leave a voicemail. He left a message asking for Rivera to call him at home that night.

*   *   *

About the same time Paul was making his phone call to Spain, Max was taking a test drive in a Nissan GT-R. He was having fun. Jake would love this car! Then he had to stop and think. Did Jake want a sports car, or did Max just assume that all teenage boys wanted sports cars because he'd wanted one when he was sixteen? He remembered timidly asking his father for a car as a high school graduation present—just a car, any car—he hadn't dared to ask for a sports car. His friends already owned cars. His father had given him a second-hand Ford just before he left for college at Duke, even though he could have easily afforded something far better. He was disappointed but he'd kept his disappointment to himself. He'd already learned by then to keep his feelings at home. But then he remembered his friend Jimmy Stinson's wreck in his Corvette; it had left him a paraplegic. His father had not deprived him; he'd only been concerned about what was best for Max. Max was always humbled by thoughts of his father, his devoted and responsible father.

He pulled into the driveway in front of the showroom and

handed the key to the salesman. At 85,000 dollars, the car wasn't cheap. He should make sure he knew what he was doing.

"Quite a ride, isn't she, sir?" asked the salesman.

Max grinned. "Sure is. I'll think about it, talk to my son, see what he wants."

"Well, I'll tell you what. Why don't you tell him he can have it if he lets his Dad drive it once in a while."

"Ha," Max chuckled. "He might let me drive it but his mother wouldn't! In fact, to tell you the truth, I don't think she'd let either one of us drive it. But we'll see, we'll see." He left the dealer. He really wanted to make a present of this car to Jake. He couldn't remember when he'd wanted anything so much—except maybe when he was sixteen and wanted a car like this for himself, a car his own father would not allow him to have.

CHAPTER SIXTEEN

Paul didn't want to violate the new rule he'd decided to follow in making plans for Nana. Ever since Max had asked that day at lunch what she preferred, he had determined never to plan for her again without asking what her own preferences were. But the agent in Barcelona told him he'd have to act quickly if he wanted to reserve the accommodation he chose—a suite with adjoining bedrooms at a hotel in the heart of the city. August was the month when all of Europe took annual vacations, and Spain, along with the rest of the southern part of the continent, was just about everybody's destination. He knew he'd have to act quickly if he wanted to reserve it; nevertheless, he decided he'd postpone the reservation until he checked with Nana to see if it suited her. He had told the agent he'd call back shortly.

"Hello, darling," he said into the phone. "I've got a chance to get a suite with a bedroom for each of us at Le Meridian in Barcelona. What do you think? I have to let the agent know right away—sorry to give you such short notice, but you know what it's like in August."

"Oh, Paul, that's wonderful. When do we leave?"

Paul was gratified that she sounded genuinely excited, eager to go. "Well, I haven't checked flights yet; it'll depend on the reservation. I could go down and get you—we'd fly out of Atlanta, of course. There are plenty of direct flights from here."

"Just let me know when you find out. I would only need a few days' notice."

"Right. Okay, then, dear. We'll do it. Call you back when it's arranged."

The time difference made it necessary to wait till

morning, but he decided to leave a voicemail for the agent to let him know he wanted the reservation. The second and third weeks of August would be a good time to go; it would give him time to get a good flight, for one thing, but he also had some things to do before he left, professional and personal.

He took the glass of merlot he'd been sipping to the balcony and sat down to enjoy the night sounds of the city. Every Wednesday afternoon, he and Max met for a drink at Gino's at four p.m., and this coming Wednesday, two days away, he was going to have the planned conversation with Jake about his work. He mulled over thoughts of what he might have to report to Max at Gino's about that conversation, which was to take place at lunch with Michelle. He hoped it would be a positive report. For just a fleeting moment, he thought of the awkwardness of the situation: conferring with the son, lunching with the mother, reporting to the father. It was almost funny, but not quite.

He had an appointment for a meeting tomorrow with a publisher's rep to discuss a possible book deal; if that went well, he wanted to start on the book before going to Barcelona—maybe work on it sometimes while he was there, if his activities with Nana allowed enough time. And he would have the time, he knew. With a little shadow of self-disapproval, he acknowledged the real purpose of the trip: to show Nana that she didn't want to return to Spain to live the rest of her life. He wanted her to enjoy herself—up to a point —and then he hoped she would find herself homesick for Savannah, for the slow, courteous, peaceful way of life in that small southern city that she knew so well. Thinking about the moss hanging from giant oak trees, swaying in the warm breezes, he felt a little homesick for Savannah himself. He knew Nana would hate the loud brashness of modern, secular Barcelona, not at all like the almost medieval Catholic city under Franco's rule that she had known when she was young.

The timing was perfect. Roxie's horse show was scheduled for the first week of August, and she'd insisted that he go to see her win first place with Sampson. Paul was smiling with that smile of affection one feels for the optimistic confidence of one's beloved child. *Not my child,* he reminded himself. He found he had to remind himself often, and his smile disappeared. It wasn't that he wanted Roxie to be his—it was the fact that he needed reminding that bothered him.

There had been affairs with married men in the past, men who had children. This was not the first time adultery had been involved in his sex life, but it was radically different with Max. How? He remembered the comment of one man in San Francisco many years ago when he was young. It was after a one-night stand of rather intense sex, and the man— what was his name? He couldn't remember now; he remembered only that the man was an Englishman visiting the U.S. for some business reason or other. He said, "I'm married, got four kids, and I love my wife like crazy. In fact, we've got a great sex life. I just like a bit of the strange now and then, you know?" And Paul, in that smug superior wisdom of the young, thought to himself: *Ha. You just think you're straight. I'm sure you do love your wife—it's platonic though, not erotic. No way could you spend a night as you just did and not be gay.*

In the years since then, however, he'd become less sure of that gay-versus-straight dividing line. Sex had been a part of his life ever since he was seventeen, and he'd always preferred sex with men, though he'd had sexual encounters with two or three women as well. He considered his current broader view of sexual preferences to be the product of experience and his own maturation.

Max, on the other hand, was a neophyte. For him, it was all so definitive, so either-or. Paul was his first experience. He'd never talked with Max about his sex life with Michelle —and he never would—but somehow he didn't believe it was in any way "false." One thing he did feel fairly certain of was what Max himself had said: he'd never felt *passion* like this before. Was that a sexual marker of some kind that identified Max as gay? Max believed it was so, but Paul himself felt much less certainty about such things now than he had when he was young. In almost all the liaisons he'd had with married men, at least half a dozen or so, his partner seemed happily married—like the Englishman—and only wanted some adventurous sex. The line between gay and straight had blurred long ago, and he was no longer sure that sexual activity, or even sexual desire itself, identified a person as gay or straight. People, he'd decided, were simply sexual, period.

But it wasn't Max's sexuality that concerned him now. He couldn't comfort himself by saying that poor Max was a gay man trapped in a straight marriage. It wasn't even the deception that adultery itself involved, though that was often discomfiting, especially since he had to work with Michelle every day. Sometimes he felt resentful that he was thus exposed to that discomfiture—until he reminded himself that Max had to sleep in the same bed with her every night.

No, it wasn't the deception, unpleasant as it was, that troubled him. In fact, he simply couldn't put his finger on it. All he knew that was truly different with Max was that he loved him. And it was *that*, that single stark truth, that was making *everything* different. He'd never loved before. Their love affair—for that was indeed what it was—had ignited almost instantly, love at first sight, as the saying goes. But underneath, very slowly, Paul had also come to love Michelle —and Roxie and Jake. And that love grew deeper every day. In fact, he'd found that it grew along with his love for Max. What troubled him was that it didn't seem incompatible. On the contrary, it felt natural.

He put the empty wine glass on the balcony floor beside him and tried to find again that mysterious interior quiet that city noise always brought him. But he felt instead a kind of disquiet that seemed urgent, that seemed to call upon him for some kind of decisive action that he couldn't identify. It wasn't unlike that call for decision he'd felt on the night he and Max had first made love in April, the night they'd arranged for a gallery tour, knowing they'd end up in Paul's apartment. Paul had felt then that he was called upon somehow to take some kind of preventive measure—and he couldn't—or didn't. He had the same feeling now, kind of like a muse almost, saying *Do something!* But what was he supposed to do? And why?

Love was never wrong. He'd heard that so often from sincere people, good people, many of them Christian heterosexuals, who worked in different ways for acceptance of the gay community, not just legal acceptance, but social and moral as well. "Love is never wrong." More than a platitude, it had become a mantra. No one could argue with it, not without being judgmental or bigoted. Paul himself had always believed it, though he'd never thought much about it before—never had much reason to think about it. But then, he'd never really loved anybody before, except Nana.

Nana. He wished he could talk to her, tell her everything. He wished now, and not for the first time, that she wasn't so religious, so deep into the Catholic Church with all its prohibitions. If it weren't for that, he knew she'd be able to understand it all and to help him understand. He felt a recurring sadness in the full weight of the estrangement between them that her faith demanded—because he couldn't be open with her, couldn't be honest with the only person who'd ever really mattered to him. He would die before he would ever let her find out—not because of any pain her finding out might cause him, but because of what it would do to her. He didn't want her hurt, and the knowledge would hurt her deeply, maybe even fatally. He leaned forward in his chair, staring at the flashing orange neon sign of a club in the street below, staring without seeing it, as he realized that his deception of Nana was exactly like his deception of Michelle.

He couldn't tell either of them the truth—*because* he loved them. Paul had to give up, to sacrifice, the closeness he should have had with Nana, and the honesty of friendship that he felt he should be able to have with Michelle.

Nana had once remarked, "There is always sacrifice in love." It must have struck him as truthful; otherwise, why would he have remembered it? A recent novel he'd read came to mind, a best-seller about two gay lovers who sacrificed their love for the sake of their families. It was an emotionally manipulative plot, rather transparently designed to make the reader feel anger toward the families, ignorant by no choice of their own, unknowingly the beneficiaries of the lovers' sacrifice—and by extension, anger toward anyone who would deny the lovers their right to love. Because isn't it true that love is never wrong?

He leaned back again in his chair, looking upward now toward the starlight. Whatever Nana had meant by her remark, he was sure it wasn't that. He sighed, picked up his glass, and went back inside the apartment to go to bed. He didn't know what Nana meant, and he didn't know what to do about—he would call it by its name—this vague *guilt* that he was feeling all the time now. And he wouldn't know what to do about it until he understood *why* he was feeling guilt in the first place. It was time to talk to Max about this, to bring the whole subject out into the open, the subject of Michelle, of Max's family. It was time to be honest about everything, and not just about their feelings for each other.

CHAPTER SEVENTEEN

Michelle put her coffee cup down on the dresser so hard it might have broken. "No!" she said, more emphatically than loudly. "You are not getting a sports car for Jake and that's final. Max, I mean it. Final!" What in the world was he thinking? A sports car for a sixteen-year-old boy? No way. No damn way—not *her* sixteen-year-old boy, anyway.

He lay in bed propped up on pillows, his fingers laced across his chest, looking as though he were in some kind of pout. It made her angry—really angry—just to look at him. She pulled a soft, flowered voile dress over her head, her eyes emerging above the neckline still staring at him. His face was immobile; his eyes, hooded. "I mean it, Max," she said.

Suddenly he threw aside the bedcovers and swung his feet down to the ivory carpeted floor. "I'm going downstairs for a smoke," he said, heading for the bedroom door.

"Okay. That's fine. Go kill yourself—*your* self, Max, not my child." The door closed behind him. God, she was angry—angry that he was making her his personal killjoy, but angrier still that he would even think of putting Jake in a sports car. She had to take several deep breaths to calm down, and to remind herself finally that he wouldn't do it on his own, wouldn't defy her parental right to veto. Surely not, especially knowing how strongly she felt about it.

She flicked the blond ends of her hair to frame her face, slipped her feet into the high-heeled sandals waiting for them, and left the bedroom. Surely, he wasn't downstairs smoking in front of the kids, was he? Michelle felt that she'd had about enough of Max this morning.

The kids were in the kitchen, and Gladys was already there. "Where's your father?" she asked, putting her empty cup on the counter a bit too loudly.

Gladys felt the tension enter the room and was silent. Roxie was apparently indifferent to the question, licking butter and jam from her fingertips from the last bite of her toast. Jake said, "Puffing on the patio," one side of his mouth curved up in an ironic smile.

"God!" Michelle said, grabbing her keys from the counter by her handbag as though they were trying to escape her grasp. "Roxie, have you finished eating? Are you ready to go to the stables? Let's go."

"Aren't you going to eat any breakfast?" asked Gladys.

"No," Michelle almost snapped back, then caught herself. "I'll go through Starbucks on the way to work." Trying to calm herself, she looked at Roxie. "Get your bag, baby, if you're ready."

Roxie gathered up the bag that contained her boots, hat, and riding crop, and they left together, Michelle closing the door behind them with deliberate softness.

"Hmm," mused Gladys, "wonder what that was all about."

"Who knows," said Jake. "Whatever. They'll get over it."

Michelle drove with a focused consciousness of the traffic, aware that her anger was still dominant. She glanced in the rear-view mirror: Roxie sat in the back seat, her head bobbing to the beat of something coming through headphones. She was glad she didn't have to engage in morning chatter just now; she could try to think rationally, get outside her anger. How could Max be willing to risk Jake's life? Did he not love his own son? *Okay,* she thought, *that's ridiculous*—of course, he loves Jake, and of course, he wouldn't knowingly choose to risk his life. Then what? What is he doing? He's *indulging* Jake—or trying to. And his desire to do that is so strong he doesn't even realize it's dangerous to Jake. That's it. In his mind, he *is* loving Jake. *But that's not love,* she thought, not real love. It was not a question of whether Max loved Jake—of course, he did. But it was as though he'd forgotten *how* to love him.

She sipped her coffee, coping with the morning traffic,

and allowed her thoughts some freedom. Her thinking was always more clear when she didn't drive her thoughts from an emotional engine, but allowed them autonomy, the freedom to take precedence over emotions, to come and go at their own will. She knew that it was more than just this incident about the sports car. It had been going on for weeks. And she knew it was not just anger she felt, but something worse, deeper, but she wouldn't know what she felt until she knew what she thought.

It wasn't difficult to think now that she'd given herself permission, and she realized then that she had not done so before—she had not *wanted* to think. She thought about the way Max had been spending so much time with Roxie ever since school let out for the summer, literally *playing* with her and her friends, as though he were one of them, not just out in the pool or playing volleyball, but even down in the rec room playing computer games with them. He was never upstairs in the evenings now, with her. He'd tried to spend time with Jake, too, but Jake had plans and friends of his own that didn't include his father—also, Jake liked to spend a good deal of his time alone. It struck her now that her son seemed to be more mature than his father.

It had charmed her for a while to watch him in all this play, and attempted play, with the children, but lately it had become worrisome. Why? Because the play was not just *one* way he spent time with Roxie, one among many other ways; it had become the *only* way. He had stopped parenting. She also realized with a small start that in spending all his time with the children, he was avoiding her. *Why?*

Lately, she'd been feeling so irritated, so easily annoyed. She'd thought that it was because he seldom wanted to make love any more, and when he did, it was perfunctory—almost like something on an agenda, something he had to do rather than something he spontaneously wanted to do. After the first few painful rejections, she had ceased any initiative. But she realized now that wasn't the only cause of her constant irritation. He had simultaneously begun to defer to her all decision-making, all parenting responsibility. He wasn't just being a child with his children, *he was being a child with her too.* No wonder there was no love-making.

How in God's name had this happened? But it didn't matter how. It had happened. *How* didn't matter.

Michelle felt tears filling her eyes. Her thoughts subsiding now, in a realization which seemed to have been pushing against the door of her mind, demanding admittance and being denied. It was a realization that came all at once now, not in pieces, of what had happened to her marriage, to her family, what had happened to *her.* There had been a death, a tragic death. And she hadn't noticed it happening, she had been distracted. Max, her husband, her children's father, had died. He was gone. And in his place, was this overgrown child, this overweight—despite all the time he was spending at the gym—this petulant child who smoked cigarettes and whined when he was reprimanded about it. And she realized that she did not love him anymore, this bloated and self-indulgent child. He was repugnant, and she resented him. She loved Max, the man who was her husband, the man who was not only the father *of* her children, but a father *to* them, as well. She loved Max, the man—and he was gone. What she had been feeling was indeed much deeper than anger; it was pain. And what she felt now was grief.

Michelle let the tears roll down her cheeks and brushed them aside with her fingers. She glanced up at the rear-view mirror and saw her daughter staring back at her, wide-eyed, the headphones dropped around her neck. Her tears were frightening her child. She tried to smile. "It's okay, baby. Mom's just been having a little tantrum."

* * *

Max padded back up the stairs in his bare feet and pajamas. Michelle had probably seen him smoking outside, where the children could see him through the glass doors. That had probably made her even angrier than she'd been upstairs. Why had she been such a bitch lately?

With some guilt, he thought he should probably have sex with her more often. It occurred to him then that when he thought of Michelle, he thought of "having sex," but when he thought of Paul, he thought of "making love." So many things were different now that he knew he was gay.

There was a lot he didn't understand yet, but he knew that it was all a matter of his own acceptance of himself as he was—and somehow, he'd also have to accept the way the nature of his marriage to Michelle was altered—probably at least until the children were grown. He pushed aside any thought of having a dreaded conversation with her: After all, he didn't know what would happen in the future; he couldn't think about the future. All his joy, all that really mattered to him now was in the present. Of course, he loved his kids, and whatever happened, he'd put them first—somehow. Meanwhile, he knew he should be more concerned about Michelle's needs.

She was probably right about the car, but he wondered what Paul would think. He decided to take Paul for a test drive and see what he thought. He might agree with Max that Jake should have the car.

CHAPTER EIGHTEEN

On Wednesday morning, Paul expected Michelle to want a little conversation alone with him before Jake arrived. He was supposed to come in around eleven, and it was already past 10:30. Finally, he buzzed her office.

"Hey, it's 10:40. Jake's coming at 11:00, right? By the way, how's he getting here?"

"He uses public transport—he's used to it, and he's good at it—better than I am. I can never figure it out."

"Well, you want to talk a little bit before he gets here?"

"Yeah—yeah, I guess so. I'll come over in a minute."

"Okay. I just thought we'd sort of confer a bit first. By the way, I want to go with you on the tour, get a feel for how he responds to different things." He lifted his finger from the intercom button. He was mildly concerned about Michelle lately. She had little downward lines at the corners of her mouth and a constant frown line between her brows.

* * *

Michelle sighed and leaned forward on the plate glass top of her desk, reflexively careful to set her elbows on the laminate section to avoid smudges. She had felt a wave of dread in the last twenty-four hours, as though tragedy were threatening to appear on the horizon, slowly approaching her and those she loved, and there was nothing she could do to stop it. There was no way for her to change anything. She knew that if her family were to be saved, it couldn't be because *she* had saved them. She had lain awake all night, trying to figure out when it began and she couldn't tell. She only knew—and of this she was certain—it depended completely on Max. Even if there were something she herself could do, she knew that her doing it was not the answer. It had to come from him. Anything more from her was not only impossible, but somehow contradictory.

She looked around her, at her office. She loved her job. She loved her family. There ought to be a different word, she thought, a different word for the love she had for her family. *My job is what I do—I love what I do—but my family is who I am, not what I do. It would grieve me to lose my job, but it would destroy me to lose my family. There ought to be a different word for it, not just "love," a word too frail....*

She had never felt so helpless, never realized how dependent she really was on another person—on Max. It was his quiet and solid strength that had bound them all together without their knowing it. She could take on many paternal responsibilities for Max—indeed, she had been doing that, it was the cause of her fatigue and her loneliness. *But I am limited—I cannot love me for you, Max.*

She pressed her mother's number on the speed dial of her cell phone.

"Hi, honey." Her mother answered on the first ring.

"Hi, Mom. Listen, dear, I don't have time to talk right now, but I wanted to ask you if it's okay if I come down to visit—just for one night, maybe leave here Friday. Is that okay? Do you have any plans?"

"No, I don't have any plans. You come any time you want to. Michelle, is anything wrong? Are the kids all right?"

The sincerity of her mother's concern, its instinctiveness, almost made tears come into her eyes. It felt so good, so surprisingly good, to *feel* someone caring for her, for her children, reflexively, naturally—not because they *should* care, but simply because they did, because she was loved. Whatever happened, she would never take such love for granted again.

"Oh, don't worry, Mother," she said. "We're all fine. I just need a little private talk with you. I can't say more now, but don't worry—we're all fine. I'll see you Friday night—I'll call you later when I know what time I'm leaving on Friday morning. Got to go right now. Love you."

She hung up, leaned back in her chair, and looked down at her left hand resting on the deep blue leather arm of the chair. Her wedding band—seventeen years old; the chair, eleven years old. She'd landed the job at Hunter Gallery eleven years ago, right after Roxie was born. The board had given her *carte blanche* to decorate her office, and the chair had been very expensive. She looked up in front of her and saw Max standing there in her memory, his eyes almost misty with pride in her, telling her that the chair matched her eyes....

She'd brought Roxie in to work with her—her cradle was set right by that chair. She couldn't bear to leave her at home, not even with her own mother—she couldn't bear to be parted from her. And everything stopped when Roxie needed to be fed, when Roxie cried—everything stopped. She continued bringing Roxie to work until her crawling made work impossible. Michelle had never been confused about priorities, not once. She loved her job, but she had always known that the person she was, including the person who loved this job, was not just Michelle, but Michelle *Maxwell*. She wished that she could believe she'd gotten confused, maybe put her job ahead of her family. She wished she could believe that whatever was happening had been her fault somehow, so that it would be something she could correct, could change. But this was not about her, and she knew it. It was not her problem to solve. They had, all of them, always depended on Max—the monolith that held them together, the *Maxwell* that made them all one together. And if they were to survive, they had to survive that way. It was what they were—all of them, including her.

"Hi." Jake came through the glass door, smiling.

"Hey, baby. Ready for the grand tour?"

"Sure. Let's do it."

She stood and pressed the intercom button. "Paul, Jake's here. You said you wanted to go with us?"

"Yes," he answered, wondering why she'd never come in to talk first. "Does he drink coffee?"

"Yes, he does," she answered, and glanced across to Jake. "You want some coffee?"

"Yeah, thanks."

"We'll meet you in the kitchen."

They met in the little office kitchen where the coffee machine was kept. Paul brought the gallery guide with him. He was animated; he'd been looking forward to this tour with Jake all morning.

"Hi!" he said, taking down the mugs hanging from hooks above the coffee machine. "You guys ready to go?"

Michelle poured their coffee while Paul looked at Jake with earnestness. "Listen, a little guidance for me here, okay? How do you feel about weaving? About pottery—things like that?"

"To tell you the truth, I don't care anything about that kind of stuff," Jake answered. "And only a little about sculpture. I guess I'm not into the three-dimensional stuff much."

"Hm. Okay. We'll just skip the third floor then."

Michelle was a little surprised, pleasantly, as they left the kitchen and headed for the elevator. She hadn't expected Paul to take over Jake's tour the way he seemed to be doing.

They walked around the watercolors and Jake appeared very interested there. Paul noticed that he read no titles, checked no prices—his interest was in the work alone. But he seemed too quiet; there were no questions or comments. Finally, Paul decided to ask questions himself. He wanted to know how Jake looked at things, how he saw them.

"What do you think of Theringer's use of multi-yellow tones here? Do you think that kind of color usage adds to the subject? To the subject *as* a basket of onions? Or maybe you think it's an abuse of color."

Jake stood with his hands tucked into the back pockets of his jeans. "Huh? Oh, I don't know." He was quiet for a moment and walked closer to the watercolor. "I guess I was just wondering why he didn't take that brownish yellow all the way to the edge of the canvas."

"Do you think he should have?" Michelle asked.

"Yeah. Yeah, I do. I mean what he wants is to show earth, isn't it? Earth doesn't end with the onion basket."

Michelle realized that Jake wasn't looking at the art in the critical terms that Paul was using. He wasn't trying to analyze the works as Paul might have done—as she herself might have done. He didn't have sufficient education for that kind of commentary, anyway. He was looking at them in terms of their execution. He was thinking about improvisation. Much as a dancer might watch a ballet.

She took the lead as Paul became silent, though he remained watchful, attentive. She revised her comments to accommodate not a critic, or even a student—but an artist. The result was interesting, if somewhat naïve. Jake became actively engaged with each piece they viewed: "Why didn't the painter lighten up a bit here? He should have. The woman's not a witch, is she?" Before an oil of wilted roses on a gray ground, he suddenly laughed and said, "All the subtlety of a sledgehammer!" She and Paul felt their way around such comments, not asking him to explain what he meant, knowing he wouldn't have the vocabulary, and knowing that certain responses to his comments might sound like a demand for an explanation he couldn't give. Michelle felt surprised and grateful for the kind of bond she and Paul seemed to form, without any effort, based on a protective understanding of Jake's unique response.

And so it went until they approached the giant canvas titled *Coeur de Lion.*

"Whoa!" said Jake. He ran his fingers through his thick blond hair, as he smiled and frowned together, and for once, went close to the painting to read the title. "Ha!" he said, striding back to Michelle and Paul. "A painting of nothing, of *absence!* Wow."

Paul couldn't resist asking, "What do you mean?"

"Well, didn't you ever see *The Wizard of Oz?* No—wait. That was the tin man, wasn't it—it was the tin man that didn't have a heart. What the lion didn't have was courage."

Paul laughed. "Okay, 'the heartless lion' instead of 'heart of the lion' then."

"All glory and no guts," Jake said.

"Well," said Michelle, "I'm just glad the artist can't hear you. This is his *magnum opus.*"

"Oh, it's okay. I just don't see much *magnum* in the *opus*, I guess. Now—what would have been neat, really worth doing, would have been to really do what he says he's done and didn't—to paint the lion's heart. But he didn't do it at all, not at all."

Michelle and Paul looked at each other. They could tell that they were both thinking the same thing. Finally, Michelle asked, "Well, what do you think the artist means by showing the 'nothing' at the center?"

Jake was silent for a long time as he stared at the painting, his arms folded and his brows furrowed. "I don't know. I mean, the whole thing is this kind of massive *glory*—you know? But there's just a void where the heart is supposed to be. No center. Like it's form without substance. So maybe that's what he meant. How do I know what he meant? It's empty."

They went to lunch at a burger place near the metro station and chatted about some of the works in the gallery that had impressed Jake the most. He had promised to take Roxie to the movies in the afternoon, so he had to leave as soon as lunch was over.

On the way back to the gallery, Michelle thanked Paul for going with them on the tour, for talking to Jake and eliciting responses from him. Then she asked, "So—what do you think?"

"Oh, he sees like an artist. I think we know that. And his work shows skill, even talent, but whether he's willing to do what it takes to develop that, there's no way to tell. That wouldn't depend on his talent...."

"No," she answered, "not on his talent, but on his heart—does he love it enough? And for that, we'll just have to wait and see."

CHAPTER NINETEEN

Max sat at Gino's waiting for Paul to arrive at four that afternoon. He knew Paul had been excited about taking Jake on a tour of the gallery, and he waited in pleasant anticipation for Paul's report, twirling his glass between his palms with a little smile on his lips. Paul really loved Jake and Roxie, and that made Max love him more. And although Michelle was seldom mentioned, he knew Paul liked her a great deal and respected her. It was the question of Michelle that made the smile disappear, the question of Michelle that would, he suspected, be the catalyst for a turning point in their relationship. They were going to have to talk about her, but that conversation couldn't happen until they knew where they were going.

Max thought the time had come for him to "come out." He thought it was time to be honest—first, about himself, and then he had to be honest about his love for Paul. He was not ashamed of it; it was the most beautiful thing in his life, and he wanted it to continue forever—until death. In the past few weeks, he'd done a lot of reading about homoerotic love and he felt he was very well-informed on the topic now—though he'd never been uninformed, exactly, in the past. He'd just never had a reason before for the strong interest he'd had lately.

Homosexuality, he knew, was inborn. No one was able to prove that, but there was no reason not to believe it—some people were just born gay and others were born straight. It had been misunderstood in the past as a "deviance," even as a "perversion," the same way people had once regarded left-handedness. People tend to fear that which they don't understand, but Paul had taught him by his own example to be tolerant toward homophobia. Some of the people he'd met through Paul—gay people—were understandably angry at a society that rejected them, ridiculed them, even condemned them. But Paul himself was not like that. He had no anger; he said there was no reason to be angry unless you didn't fully accept yourself the way you are—and that made sense to Max. It was a matter of self-acceptance; once that was truly accomplished, the anger disappeared, to be replaced by patience and understanding toward people who were, for one reason or another—usually cultural reasons, sometimes religious—unable to accept people whose sexuality was different from their own.

Max had never been homophobic. He'd always believed in gay rights—the right to live a normal life, free from discrimination, free to work, marry, and have children—usually by adoption, sometimes by surrogates. He had a momentary fantasy of a child that he and Paul might have together, a sibling for Jake and Roxie. He knew Paul would be a great parent. Most of what he had read about homosexuality was not really new to him, except some of the historical statistics—he'd never been aware before, for example, of the homosexuality of many great historical figures. They'd had to keep their sexual orientation a secret to protect themselves from a condemning society, and that was tragic. But things were changing now. There was no reason now to be secretive.

It was time. Max felt that his self-acceptance was complete. It was time now, but when he tried to imagine himself making the announcement to his family, he found that he couldn't. The ground under his feet seemed to become unstable. He yearned to honor his love for Paul, he yearned to end this life of duplicity. They must decide *together* what they wanted for their future. That had to be done first. Then, he felt certain, Roxie and Jake would accept him as gay. It would be a little difficult, but only because it meant looking at their Dad a little differently. They had been raised to be tolerant toward people who are different, and he had no real fear of losing their love or respect. They'd need time to process it, but he knew it would be okay. When he thought of how this would affect his children, he felt some measure of fear, but he knew it would not alter their relationship in any really destructive way. Michelle, however, was another matter.

Since his self-discovery, he remembered all the times in the past when he'd admired—and even been *moved* by—male beauty. He understood that emotional response now to be unrecognized arousal. There was so much he understood about himself now that he'd just never thought about before —his repressed emotionalism, repressed spontaneity. And his belief, probably instilled in him when he was too young to evaluate it, that being a man meant loving a woman—loving her erotically—having children to protect and care for with her, that care and protection illogically extending to her, and inhibiting her full personhood. It was actually something he'd read about lesbian love that had enlightened him: If that was what being a man was, what did that mean for lesbian love? He realized that he'd had prejudices in the past of which he wasn't even aware. Self-acceptance was not an instantaneous thing—it took time, a slow, step-by-step deconstruction of past errors in his thinking, deconstructing a belief system he hadn't even been aware of until he discovered he was gay.

Michelle was irritable, and she drank too much. She'd always seemed to him to be distracted. He wondered now if he had not perhaps inadvertently, through no fault of his own, kept her from the sexual fulfillment she might have had with a heterosexual man. He didn't know, he couldn't know, but he was convinced that she deserved someone else, someone who was not gay. She'd be happier without him, he thought, not just sexually, but in all ways—free to be the strong and confident woman she was. It would be difficult, traumatic, for her at first, but in the longer view, she'd be glad—she'd be a happier, more fulfilled person. All of this had to be discussed with Paul.

Most of all, he knew enough at this point to know that the life he was leading had to change. There was no integrity in it. He didn't like deception—he knew Paul didn't like it, and he was convinced that Michelle herself would not like it if she knew about it. He'd decided he would bring it up today, and not wait any longer. They had to discuss it, to make plans, to settle things first between themselves, and then with others. They must make decisions together—as a couple.

Paul wove his way through the tables toward Max, to the table by the window where they always sat. He approached Max from behind and put his hand on Max's shoulder, leaned down as if to speak in his ear and brushed his cheek with a kiss instead. The first time he'd done that made Max feel that he'd almost burst with joy and pride—it was an *almost* overt sign, a *nearly* public declaration that they were lovers. Paul sat down in the armchair facing Max, leaned back, and loosened his tie. He was smiling—the tour must have gone well.

A waiter arrived, bringing Paul his customary bourbon over cracked ice. "Good afternoon, Mr. Meyer," he said, placing the drink on the little table between them. He picked up Max's glass. "Can I get you another one, sir?"

Max nodded. "So," he said to Paul. "How did it go?"

"Your son is an artist, Max." Paul was almost grinning. He talked a little then about how Jake had responded to the art, at least to those pieces that interested him—he'd instinctively improvised, changed, altered them in some way. He had a lot of learning to do, Paul said, and there was no way to know whether his interest would continue, but if it did, he might be an artist someday.

Max was pleased. "Just think, Paul. If these were other times—or maybe if Jake had a different father—a straight man for a father, maybe even a homophobic one—he wouldn't get the encouragement he'd need. He would probably be pressured to go into law like his dad, or some other 'masculine' kind of field. And maybe the world would lose a great artist."

"Oh, I think you're stretching it a bit, Max. Good grief—there are many great artists in history who were mostly straight—and had straight fathers."

"Well, we don't know that, do we?" said Max. "Who knows now about a lot of things? History has been written by straight people, you know."

Paul laughed a little but then he made a little frown. "Listen, my love. Don't drown in all that stuff you're reading. You can drown in it, you know. Keep some perspective. Falling in love with a man does not justify re-writing all of history—even if you decide to re-write your own history—and I'm not even sure you should do that much."

"I don't know. Maybe you should do some reading yourself. Anyway, I want to tell you about what I want to do for Jake's birthday. What do you think about a sports car?"

"*What?* Does he want a sports car?"

"Of course he does. Every kid wants a sports car."

"Wow. That's quite a—a surprise, for a sixteen-year-old anyway. What does Michelle think about it?"

"Oh, well, she thinks he's still a little kid, you know. He's not. He's a young man now—but she's doing her Mommy thing. Let's finish our drinks and go take a test drive. It's a beauty—the color is called 'chrome yellow.' Wait till you see it."

"Have you got time?"

"Yeah. I'm at the gym for an extended session this afternoon. I left a voicemail."

* * *

Late that night, around midnight, Paul sat on his balcony, his feet up on the railing, ankles crossed, his hands in the pockets of his robe. He couldn't sleep. They'd gone for a ride in the chrome yellow sports car. Max was like a kid himself, like a sixteen-year-old kid. It had been fun, but Paul had trouble imagining Jake in the driver's seat where Max was. The image didn't match the Jake he'd gotten to know a little better that morning at the gallery.

They had come back to the apartment and made love, playful, almost like children, reminding Paul of his first adolescent encounters—yet that very reminder evoked a strange feeling of distance in Paul. He felt suddenly very old, remote from Max. He'd had the same sensation while Max was driving the sports car. Max's childlike happiness was endearing, yet vaguely troubling.

Afterwards, they'd sat together on the balcony. Max was smoking. He wanted to talk, he said. He thought it was time they talked about their future—he didn't say "about Michelle and the kids;" instead, he'd said "the future." Paul had been ready for that conversation for some time, but he thought they had to discuss Michelle first; he didn't think there was a future *until* they talked about Michelle.

It was almost two o'clock in the morning, and Paul had finally got out of bed and come outside for fresh air, fresh thinking. And he thought he finally understood now why he'd been unable to talk to Max the way Max had wanted: Max wanted to talk about *them*, to make big decisions about *them*—and then he wanted any talk about his family to be a consequence of, dependent upon, decisions they made about themselves.

Paul had felt very uncomfortable with that line of thought, and he knew now that was the reason he'd been unable to deal with it as Max had wanted. He was remembering Michelle, the way he'd seen her that morning in the gallery. What she did was very far from any "Mommy thing." He'd seen her calmly detach herself from any emotional response to Jake in order to objectively assess his interest; he'd seen her deliberately avoid saying anything that might be understood as "encouragement." Paul had the odd and uncomfortable feeling that he understood her better than her husband did, and worse—it seemed to him that he felt more protective of Jake than his father.

It was just such sensations as these that had made him believe a few days ago that he and Max had to discuss Michelle openly—because they never did. The conviction had nothing to do with their own relationship, but with Michelle and the children. And, ironically, it was the same sensations, more amplified now than before, that had made it impossible to have that discussion.

CHAPTER TWENTY

Michelle sat with her mother, Laura, in the little courtyard garden behind Laura's condominium in St. Augustine. Warm breezes from the Atlantic wafted over the ivy-covered brick wall, moving the leaves of a giant philodendron in the corner. They were silent; the only sounds were the tinkling of a small fountain under the philodendron and the rhythmic swashing of the distant surf. It was dusk; the muted landscape lighting in the little garden came on, giving just enough light to illuminate the profiles of the two women in a soft silhouette. Michelle looked down at her wine glass on the lacy top of the little black wrought iron table; she twirled the stem between her fingers. She had managed, to her surprise, to say it all—even the part about the sex—without crying, and the lump in her throat, which had once or twice made it almost impossible to speak, was gone. She felt empty—and almost drowsy—now that it was all out, as though she wanted to sleep now, to rest after a long period of being too alert, too anxious, tense.

"He's having an affair," Laura said bluntly.

Michelle blinked. In an instant she knew it was true. In another instant, Shorty's Gym and Fitness Center came to mind—yet Max had not lost a single pound—and the unusual dinner meetings with clients.

Her mother was watching her face. "Don't get curious, Michelle. It will only make it worse, and it might even be dangerous. It doesn't matter who it is."

She met her mother's level gaze. "What am I supposed to do?"

"*Do?* Nothing. You wait."

There was a silence then for a moment while Michelle tried briefly—but only briefly—to argue in her mind.

"How do you know that, Mother? How can you be so sure?"

"Oh, honey," Laura declared. "It's textbook. Downright classic."

It dawned on Michelle then that her mother's certainty could only be the result of experience. "It's hard for me to believe that Dad—"

"You're not being realistic, dear. Few marriages last forty-seven years without at least one infidelity, probably more. Now don't get distracted. Your father is not the issue here." She paused for a moment while Michelle re-directed her thoughts. "All you need to think about now is your role. And your role is to have *no* role in any part of it. You're an exclusion."

"Oh, God—that's just how I feel. That's what's so painful. I feel as though I've been *excluded* from my own marriage." The lump came back to her throat. She sipped her wine to swallow it down.

"You have. But that's a good thing for you now. I don't know how serious it is, but if it's serious at all, you need to be as invisible as you can. The more visible you are, the more a problem you'll become—and problems have to be solved. Don't be a problem, honey—that's the *worst* thing that could happen for you now." Michelle shuddered as anger subsided into fear—as the unthinkable became possible and yielded to something even more unthinkable.

Michelle went to bed that night aware only of being drained and exhausted. She slept soundly for the first time in over a week, at least. It was deep and restful, dreamless, and the next morning at breakfast, she felt stronger. She wondered why she herself had never even thought of having an affair. Her mother said it wasn't because she was good, moral, or righteous—though she believed her to be all those things. It was because she was *sensible.*

"All the Pennington women are sensible, Michelle. That's the real reason there's never been a divorce in our family.

You're married to a Decatur Maxwell, but you're a South Carolina Pennington, born and bred. You know, divorce wasn't even legal in South Carolina until 1948. Not so much because we believe that divorce is morally wrong. I think it was mostly because there just wasn't enough need for it in South Carolina. We had other ways of solving marital problems."

Heading back north now on I-95, she thought about her mother with gratitude. When Jake was born, Max had been with her, but afterward, when she lay in pain and exhaustion, it was her mother she had wanted. She smiled now, remembering her mother coming into the hospital room, singing a country song: *"Sometimes it's hard to be a woman...."* And Michelle had laughed, even though it hurt to laugh, and she'd answered in a made-up line, "...but thank God we're made of elastic!" She smiled at the memory; it felt good to smile again, even if it wouldn't last long. She heaved a great sigh: there was nothing she could do—but wait. It was Max's problem and he'd have to solve it—not her. And if he couldn't solve it—well, she'd deal with that disaster when it came. She was too tired for worry now, for anger; too tired for anything beyond simple endurance.

* * *

In Paul's apartment in Atlanta, Max scruffled around on the nightstand to find his crumpled pack of cigarettes, sat up in bed and lit one. He twirled it between his fingers, watching the smoke ascend in a steady upward stream. Michelle hated his smoking. True, he was overweight and his blood pressure was creeping up. "You're burning up your entire cardio-vascular system every time you light up one of those damned things!" she'd yelled at him, standing there in the kitchen, her hands on her hips, watching him head outside to the pool to smoke. But the nagging only made him want a cigarette all the more.

Paul hated it too, and for the same reason Michelle had

so often and so forcefully expressed. "You're killing yourself," he'd said. "You do know that, don't you?" But Paul had another reason for despising Max's smoking, one he'd expressed only once, and for Max, that once was enough: "You know, Max, you already have lines coming around your mouth. You're going to have one of those anus-mouths you see on old people who've smoked all their lives. And it stinks, you know. It's a repulsive habit, disgusting, actually." He looked at the burning end of the cigarette he held now between his thumb and forefinger, twirling it and watching the smoke. Why was that second reason so much more potent than the first? The first only made him want to smoke more; the second, while it didn't kill the craving, had a compelling force. Why? But, as always, he didn't answer his own question.

He didn't smoke it. He snuffed it out in the ashtray on the nightstand and turned to look at Paul, who watched him snuff out the cigarette with a mischievous little smile and a twinkle in his dark eyes, but he said nothing. Max fell back against the pillow, his heart so full of the mischievous little smile that he thought it would burst. How is it, he asked himself, that a smile can be so excruciatingly adorable? He had to go. He had to pick Roxanne up at the stables and he was already late.

"You have to go, don't you," Paul said quietly. "It's okay, you know, more than okay. Some things are more important than other things. That's always true, not just now or here, but always and everywhere."

Max sat up again and swung his legs over the side of the bed. "You know," he began slowly, almost as if he were talking to himself, not looking at Paul. "Jake wouldn't give a damn one way or the other. Not really." He slipped his polo tee-shirt over his head and headed for the mirror to comb his hair. "Roxanne's the only one I'd be concerned about. Eleven is a tender age for little girls, especially now that puberty has arrived." He paused deliberately, pretending to be concerned with his hair. Then he took a deep breath and continued, still not looking at Paul: "As for Michelle—well, to tell you the truth, I think she'd be relieved." Paul had kept silent; Max finally mustered enough courage to look at him in the mirror, preparing himself for anything but what he saw: shock. Paul looked as though Max had struck him.

"Oh, well," Max said quickly, lightly, "what the hell." He strode rapidly to the bedside and gave Paul a quick kiss on a face that had turned to stone. "I'll try to call you tomorrow if I can. If not, I'll talk to you Monday." Paul made no reply; he remained frozen, staring past Max as he left.

Dammit, Max thought on his way down to the parking garage. He wished he hadn't said what he did, though he'd thought about it so many times that it had to come out sooner or later. That look on Paul's face—what did it mean? There had never been any mention, not even indirectly, of the possibility of Max separating from his family. But surely it had occurred to Paul, too. How could it not have occurred to him? The subject had to be dealt with somehow. Whatever they decided to do—and Max knew it would have to be decided together—it would have to begin by bringing it out into the open between them. Sooner or later, they'd have to talk about it. But the look on Paul's face had frightened him. He would never say anything about it again—he couldn't now. He didn't dare bring it up; he'd have to wait for Paul to do that now. *God! The look on his face. You'd think it was his family and I was the one wanting him to leave.* For the first time, it didn't charm him to think of Paul's attachment to the kids. He beeped the keychain to unlock the Lexus and walked rapidly to the car. Paul worked with Michelle every day. Max knew he thought very highly of Michelle—did he now think more highly of her than he did of Max? Then the absurdity of the situation struck him: Was he jealous of his own wife? He slammed the door of the car, started the engine, and took off with far too much speed for a parking garage. He forced himself to slow down—he had the sensation again of drowning, of not knowing which way to go in order to come up for air.

PART III

AUGUST

CHAPTER TWENTY-ONE

Paul and Michelle sat at the large conference table in Paul's office with representatives of half a dozen Atlanta art organizations. Most of them would likely play a very small part in the project Paul had planned for exhibitions of local amateur art, but in arranging the meeting, he could hardly afford to risk offending any one of them, so they were all invited. What the project would need more than anything else was their support, their *enthusiastic* support. The fact that they were not all prestigious would have to be ignored. The rest of the table was filled with art teachers from local schools, and finally, faculty representatives from the art departments of several colleges and universities in Atlanta.

The large table was full; extra chairs had to be brought in, and the room was almost uncomfortably crowded, especially since a buffet table had been set up at one end of it for refreshments—coffee and tea, juice and pastries. Paul wasn't bothered by the close quarters everyone had to suffer; he knew that it gave the meeting an ambiance of informality and encouraged cooperation by forced mutual familiarity. They had actually been able to make a good deal of progress that might not have been expected in a more formal setting.

Michelle was deeply impressed. The project would be a major public relations coup for Hunter Gallery. And it would do more than anything else to restore the gallery to its original mission of encouraging young artists, a mission that had been lost by its former director, who'd been far more concerned with financial solvency and avoided taking chances with unknown artists. She sat next to Paul taking notes, fascinated by the enthusiasm that emanated from everyone and by Paul's deft handling of the agenda of this first meeting. He kept everyone on track while simultaneously avoiding any appearance of discouraging the spontaneous expression of ideas, questions, and even humorous references to the close quarters.

The meeting was a success. Sponsored by Hunter Gallery, which would function only in an umbrella capacity, several small competitions over the course of a year would take place in various locations throughout Atlanta, culminating in the clearance of the ground floor of the gallery to exhibit the winning pieces and offer them for sale. It would be a huge boost for local amateur artists. It would give them a chance to have their work evaluated, a venue to gain public notice, and the opportunity to receive payment for their work.

This first meeting was devoted to establishing an overall structure of the project. All the representatives would return to their respective associations to establish their own internal organization. How clever of Paul, Michelle thought, to make sure that Hunter's responsibility remained limited to its umbrella function, avoiding all the inevitable conflicts that were bound to happen within the local groups. Yet he'd established the project from its beginning as "The *Hunter* Celebration of Young Artists." Brilliant.

The meeting was winding down, people were departing, full of ideas and plans. The next meeting was scheduled for mid-September, and in the meantime, Hunter would have no responsibility other than to arrange that meeting. Michelle, Paul, and the secretary, Lolly, were removing napkins, disposable coffee cups and plates and replacing the folding chairs into the storage closet. Michelle reminded Paul that she had to leave in order to take Roxie to the doctor, and apologized for leaving them with the rest of the clean-up. He had been concerned, timidly asking whether something was wrong, whether Roxie was okay. It made her smile to think about how Paul was almost embarrassed by his concern. He had become "Uncle Paul" to the kids, in the way that such a name often suggested the close friend of a family, though neither of the kids called him "uncle." They were almost as fond of him as he seemed to be of them, especially Roxie, who sometimes called him her "boyfriend."

Michelle assured him that Roxie was fine; she only needed a check-up. But the truth was that Roxie had turned out to be her mother's daughter in a particularly unfortunate way: apparently, she was going to have horrific periods. She'd had only one full period since the onset of puberty, but it was probably portentous. Michelle had recognized all the signs of the pre-menstrual syndrome she'd suffered in her youth, but in Roxie's case, she thought it might be even worse. And when her period came, it was very heavy—almost alarmingly so—and Roxie had spent a full day in bed with an elevated temperature, painful cramps, and bloating. Over-the-counter medication hadn't helped much, so Michelle made an appointment with Dr. Stratham to discuss possible amelioration of the discomfort. The horse show was scheduled right in the middle of her next period, and Roxie was terrified that she might not be able to compete.

Michelle drove through the Atlanta traffic, which she hated, and determined again to get Jake to show her the intricacies of the public-transit system. He'd agreed to do it, but she kept putting it off, letting other things take precedence. It seemed to her now that her life was a constant negotiating of "traffic." In one way or another, the children had occupied almost all her concern lately, with only a small part left over for her job, and no part at all for herself. And Max—well, Max had become almost a nonentity. She was no longer angry about his abdication, only sad, and glad that at least for now, the children occupied her time and thoughts.

Jake had gone camping with some friends. In the end, he'd declared that he wasn't really interested in going fishing in Alaska with Max and Paul. He wasn't "into all that fishing and hunting stuff," he'd said. But he loved nature, the woods and the wilderness, especially in the mountains north of

Atlanta. One of his friends was an enthusiastic amateur photographer and Jake wanted to learn more about photography. Cecil Ferguson, the father of one of the boys, took five of them to the woods north of Chickamauga.

But this was Jake's third trip away from home since the beginning of summer, and it seemed to Michelle that even when he was home, he spent very little time with the family, and then only with her, and sometimes Roxie. She had become aware that Jake was avoiding his family—avoiding his father, actually. Max tried to be "buddies" with him, but it wasn't working. Jake had been much more comfortable with Max before his metamorphosis—back when Max was more distant from the kids, more a personification of paternal authority. Michelle had been trying to read the change in Jake's attitude toward his father. Most of all, Jake seemed *saddened. Like me,* she thought, *we both miss Max.* Roxie's slight withdrawal could be understood as a consequence of the onset of maturation, but not Jake's.

The tension and irritability that came from her anxiety before she visited her mother had subsided completely now, replaced by resignation. Her concern now was how all of this —this "problem" (she chose not to name it as "infidelity")— was affecting the kids. She didn't think about how it affected her, physically or psychologically, but she knew it was changing her. Sometimes she reflected philosophically on how a change in one's spouse created not only a change in the marriage, but in the entire personality of oneself. She was always distracted now, always "somewhere else," and she craved solitude. She saw in herself the same personality traits she'd been concerned about in her son.

She pulled into the driveway, stopped the car, and went up the steps into the kitchen. Gladys was there. "Hi," she said. "How's Roxie?"

Gladys was polishing silver and shrugged with a little frown: "Well, Mrs. Maxwell, she's lying down. This isn't like her, I don't think. And her period's not even here yet. I asked her."

"No, it's not like Roxie at all. And the long-range view isn't good for our little girl, I'm afraid. I think she's worse than I was—and it was bad for me. I hope the doctor has something to help. Nowadays they have medications they didn't have when I was a girl."

"I'd be careful about some of that stuff if I was you."

"Don't worry. I'll be careful. I'm not letting her have anything until I've researched it first."

She went upstairs to get Roxie. The house seemed so quiet. Gladys had the kitchen television going and all her silver-polishing things scattered around; it almost seemed that Gladys was the only sign of life. A now-familiar wave of loneliness washed over her.

CHAPTER TWENTY-TWO

Max had continued reading about homosexuality in spite of Paul's cautionary remarks about it. He'd read an interview with Johnny Pepper, a rather famous motivational speaker for gay men. He didn't subscribe to any of the magazines because he didn't want them coming to the office or the house, and he never read such publications online because he didn't want to download them, not even to his own laptop. Instead, he bought printed publications at a newsstand, read when he had the opportunity, and discarded them afterwards.

He'd found the interview with Pepper very encouraging about the importance of 'coming out.' Stopping short of any reference to religion—except for the occasional approving reference to the Episcopal Church, which was Max's own church—the interview had an almost evangelical tone, with Pepper sounding much like a preacher. It was, or so Pepper believed, a matter of "morality," which Pepper interpreted primarily as honesty: one must be honest with oneself and with others. It was the deceit that was "sinful." Pepper even used the word "unmanly." But most of all, it was a matter of duty, a "sacred" obligation to fulfill oneself as God had made him. The interview was full of missionary zeal.

Max knew that Johnny Pepper was right. The thought of coming out to his family was terrifying, but he knew he would find the strength to do it, if he could only count on Paul's support. And so far, that support was not there. Paul was evidently satisfied with things as they were. Max asked himself increasingly often, and with increasing self-pity, whether Paul knew what the clandestine nature of their relationship cost him, not just in the lack of freedom to be with Paul as he knew he should be, but in his own loss of self-respect. Although he didn't think of adultery in explicitly religious terms, he did feel its effects on his self-esteem. What was "wrong" about what they were doing wasn't the adultery, as such, but the dishonesty of it—especially since it required Max to play the part of a straight husband, something he now knew he was not. At least, he was pretty sure of that, if not absolutely certain.

More than once, he'd thought with sadness about the intimacy he'd shared with Michelle in the past, though he couldn't tell whether it was grief or nostalgia. And more than once, he'd thought about the times when the family were all together, especially on the houseboat—for some reason, being on the houseboat together amplified this feeling—a feeling of "rightness" that their unity brought him. Michelle was a natural mother; her intelligence and successful career notwithstanding, he knew that she was, to the core of her being, a mother. And he, Max, in an almost mystical homeostasis, was a father—at least until recently.

His fatherhood felt awkward to him now, as though it were no longer natural to him, and he believed that this too was a consequence of the involuntary estrangement from his children that his deceit entailed. He would have to become acquainted with his children anew as a gay man; meanwhile, he was trying to become their friend in order to compensate for the deceit. And it was because he could not be honest with Michelle that he avoided being alone with her as much as possible—yet he could not say that the few occasions they'd made love since the beginning of his affair with Paul had been disappointing or unsatisfactory in any way; it was the deceit that was making *everything* awkward.

He had secretly explored this new-found sexuality with pornography. It wasn't so much for arousal or gratification as for trying to understand himself. He found, to his confusion, that he was as much aroused by one kind of sex as the other; he'd wondered then if that kind of vicarious arousal wasn't just the thrill of participating in something forbidden. When he couldn't understand the bi-sexual nature of the arousal, he stopped looking at the pornography altogether. It clarified nothing for him. He decided that his love for Paul, his passion for him, was enough to inform him of who and what he was. And he was gay.

He had finally given up all the reading, realizing, as Paul had said, that very little of it had much to do with him personally; it seemed either too clinical or too extreme—even bizarre. He lay in bed now, reading a best-selling thriller. Michelle was sitting at her dressing table in a bathrobe, massaging cream on her elbows and ankles. He asked her what Dr. Stratham had said about Roxie's severe periods.

"She recommended birth control pills. I thought she might do that; I think it's pretty standard now to treat difficult periods with hormones. Seems odd, though—Roxie on the pill."

"What's wrong with that? She wouldn't be taking it for birth control, just to make her periods easier."

"Yes, I know. But it's—I don't know—sort of like pretending something isn't so."

"What do you mean?"

"The hormone works by making her stop ovulating."

Max was silent for a while. He knew Michelle was thinking that the drug was "unnatural," but if it helped Roxie, why not use it? "Have you asked Roxie what she thinks about it? I mean, if it helps her, she might not care if it's 'unnatural.'"

"Yes, I did talk to her. I explained the benefits and the side effects. She'd have an increased risk of breast cancer in later life if she stays on this drug. And birth control drugs often cause infertility, too, after they're discontinued. Of course, that's not a concern for her now—and long-range side effects don't matter if her use is short-term.   She's still thinking about it. Roxie's not dumb, you know."

"It sounds to me like you were trying to influence her not to take it, sounds like you're scaring her."

"No. But I think she deserves the whole truth, not just part of it. And she understood it. She'll probably take it—though it's too late now for her to make the horse show."

That was the end of the discussion. It was another instance of Max's exclusion, and he knew it. He couldn't participate in this part of his daughter's life, not as Michelle could—and did. He didn't feel any offense, any anger about that, just a kind of sad sweetness in his love for his child, his little girl—who was becoming a woman without any role for him to play in that process. He put his book aside and pulled the covers over himself, thinking, *I'm feeling now the same thing that probably countless millions of fathers have felt and will always feel—left out, left out of a big part of my little girl's life.* The feeling of sad sweetness made him almost feel like crying. He had an impression then of being a part of something incomprehensibly large and powerful, like a great river in which he moved with the current, along with millions of other people, both men and women, past and present. Not he, not anyone, could swim against that steady current, not even if they tried. It was bigger than he was, infinitely more powerful. He was just a small bit of mortal something in a great, mysterious, immortal movement. To try to fight against its force would be to drown. He had the uncomfortable idea then that his affair with Paul was actually a defiance of that force, a defiance almost pitiably weak, but far worse that that: in the great river that moved everyone, with or without their consent—he and Paul were meaningless.

Michelle got into bed, turned off her bedside lamp, and turned her back to him. She never approached him now, and he had mixed feelings about that: He was relieved, but he also felt somehow abandoned and sad.

That night he had a terrible dream. The houseboat was on a river, and a storm was tossing it violently. The children were screaming in terror, and Michelle was trying to steer the boat alone to keep it afloat, but she was losing the struggle. He woke to find himself clinging to a pillow as though it were a life raft. He wished desperately that Paul were there.

CHAPTER TWENTY-THREE

Max had to go to New York to see a client, and he had wanted Paul to go, too—separately, of course—so that they could have some time together. Max's lack of caution often worried Paul. No, it was not a good idea for him to leave town at the same time. But after Max left, he decided to go see Nana, so he was leaving town anyway. Max was angry on the phone.

"I thought you said you shouldn't be gone at the same time."

"Well, no, I shouldn't. But I don't know why you're fussing about it, Max. The only reason I'm going is that I have to see her doctor about the trip. It's not that far off, you know. I have to have all the information I need to keep her safe. Besides, she called and asked me to come. Anyway, I'm coming back tomorrow; you're not coming back till Wednesday."

Nana had indeed called and wanted him to go to Savannah—rather odd, actually, since she didn't *ask* him to visit. It was more like a command: "Paul, I want you to come down here. There's something I want to talk to you about." It was unusually imperious language for her. But that wasn't the only reason he was heading south on the interstate now. It was true that he needed to talk to Dr. Hernandez before taking Nana on a transatlantic flight to a foreign country. He needed to know her medications, whether he should take charge of them—he thought he should. He also needed to know what to do if there was an emergency, and maybe other things he didn't foresee now. But he also felt a strong need to get away—away from Max, away from the whole Maxwell family, and even away from Hunter—which had been a centrifuge of emotional chaos almost ever since he'd arrived there. So far, his tenure there had been very successful professionally; he knew that all the board members were more than happy with his performance, but his personal life had become unmanageable. He needed to *think,* not to feel.

Michelle worried Paul. He saw her through the glass door of his office, walking down the hallway a couple of days ago and was struck by her appearance, unguarded for the moment. Her head was always lowered now and her shoulders stooped, almost rounded, as if she had aged within the last couple of months. He'd noticed that her face looked puffy lately, like the face of a heavy drinker. She was very attentive to her work, but she almost never smiled now.

Did she know? No. He was certain of that. She could not possibly behave so warmly toward him if she knew. That would have been more than hypocrisy; it would've had to be some kind of malice. And Michelle was neither hypocritical nor malicious. But she knew *something.* Her look was not one of fear or suspicion, but a look of sadness, even grief.

He switched off the Mozart concerto on the radio. It was time, he thought, to acknowledge something he hadn't wanted to: He and Max were hurting her. He had no idea how Max behaved with her in private; it was still something they never talked about. But he couldn't tell himself now that Max would keep his happy marriage if only he'd behave "normally" with Michelle. That was what he'd been hoping for, he knew, though he'd never said anything to Max about it—never even really admitted it to himself. Why not? Because he actually knew very well—though he'd refused to allow himself to think about it—how unfair it was to Max, what it demanded of him. And now he acknowledged how selfish and unrealistic it was of him. And why had he held such a hope in the first place? Again, it was for his own sake —so that he would not have to feel any moral responsibility in their affair. He was filled with disgust for himself.

He was responsible for this. It was time to face that. He

was responsible for Max's dilemma, the impossible position Max was in. He was responsible, too, for Michelle's sorrow. Suddenly, almost as if it moved of its own volition, his fist hit the steering wheel so hard that he had to recoil, to draw back. Something had to be done. This couldn't go on. He was still fifty miles outside Savannah—he had fifty miles to *think* now, fifty miles before he would face Nana with the smiling innocent face of her beloved grandson.

Instantly then, as though it had entered his head to end the affair—which hadn't happened—he found himself flooded with love for Max. All his senses came alive—touch, sight, taste, sound, and smell—all came alive, alive with *Max*. At the same time, his chest tightened so that he could hardly breathe, as though his heart would actually break with love, with love that was stifling him. A memory of Max's face rose before him, how he looked that night in the gallery when they first touched and Max's face, looking at him with fear, with hope almost desperate, trembling with desire. Paul's vision blurred. He raised his fingers to his cheeks and found them wet. *Oh, God. How I do love you, Max!*

It took several minutes for his breathing to stabilize, for the tears to stop. And he had to return to thoughts of Michelle. He loved her in so many ways. As a close colleague—their shared love for art, for beauty, a critical comprehension nearly mutual; that was very rare. He loved her as a friend; they'd become so close in working together that they almost shared each other's thoughts; they could even enjoy silences together. He loved her as Roxie's mom. He always enjoyed seeing them together, doing their mother-daughter banter, especially when affection entered into it. He loved her as a sister he'd never had. He felt *kin* to her somehow, completely independent of any association either of them had with Max. Her happiness and welfare were as important to him as his own. And he was hurting her. He was destroying that happiness and welfare. How? Exactly how? *He was destroying her family.*

He felt as though he were a poison of some kind, or a disease, a fatal disease that was killing Michelle without her knowledge of it. He was killing his friend, his sister; he was killing Roxie's mom. He was hurting Max, hurting Michelle —even hurting the children. Self-loathing, remorse, pounded him. Why was this happening? Because Max was married? But, he reminded himself, he'd had affairs with married men before. A huge, contradictory *but* hit him with an impact almost physical: *but* he *knew* this wife, he *knew* these children. He hadn't known the families of the other married men—was that the reason he'd never felt this guilt? Not knowing them didn't mean they didn't exist. The only difference here was that he loved Max. He asked himself whether he felt guilty about adultery. No—not in the abstract, anyway. He was feeling this guilt only because he knew the persons affected by what he was doing—knew them personally, and loved them.

But what if he *didn't* know them? There was something deeper here, deeper than adultery—which, by itself, seemed almost irrelevant, as "mere" adultery. It was knocking quietly, almost timidly, at his conscious awareness. He had the idea that he needed to know what it was before he allowed it to enter, but then he realized, with an almost bitter ironic smile, how contradictory that idea was.

He made a conscious effort to keep his breathing steady and his mind calm as he cautiously ventured toward the thought he knew he'd been repelling: It had something to do with the business of abstract and concrete, of known persons and those unknown. And it was bigger than this particular crisis, this personal crisis of his own—much bigger. It had to do with larger "abstracts" and "concretes." He didn't know what it was, but he knew that within it lay the only real answer to his urgent question, *What should I do?*

But by then he was pulling into Savannah traffic. August tourists in the historic district meant a lot of pedestrians. He had to pay closer attention to driving now. He flipped the visor down and looked at his face in the mirror. His eyes were dry now, but they were red. He looked for a place to pull over and put some drops in his eyes and finally pulled into a parking space at a convenience store. Checking his glove compartment, he found no eye drops, so he went inside the store and bought a small bottle of Visine, but when he came back to his car and started to put the drops in his eyes, he found that his hands were shaking too violently. He had to sit there, very still, watching people going in and coming back out of the store—so free from the turmoil that was consuming him, sitting there in the parked black Mercedes behind tinted glass, waiting, waiting to calm down enough to erase the red from his eyes with eye drops, waiting for a painless answer, waiting for a miracle.

CHAPTER TWENTY-FOUR

Jake was back from his camping trip, but Michelle had seen little of him until dinner on Monday. He'd taken Roxie to the movies on Sunday afternoon, and Sunday night some of his friends came over. They played computer games in the rec room downstairs until after Michelle had gone to bed, so she didn't have much time with him except during dinner on Sunday evening. Max was in New York—not due back until Wednesday—and Michelle was rather looking forward to having a couple of evenings alone with the kids. Unfortunately, however, Paul had gone to Savannah to visit his grandmother, and it seemed that one crisis after another happened at the gallery that day, when there was no one there to help her deal with things. The board's auditor had found a mistake she'd made on the tax forms. Nothing serious, but it took several hours to find out where she'd gone wrong and fix the problem. And of course, that would be the time when Mrs. Johansen decided she didn't want that montage she'd bought, after all, so there was that paperwork to deal with. She was interrupted so many times revising the tax forms that she'd had to stay late to finish them. She was tired at dinner.

"Mom, are you tired? You look really dragged out." Jake said.

"Yes, honey, I am. Paul had to go to Savannah to see his grandmother today, and so, naturally, all sorts of little problems waited until today to come up." She was drinking her fourth glass of Chardonnay, after she'd promised herself never to have any more than two glasses at a time.

"Guess what, Jake. Mom's going to give me birth control pills!" Roxie grinned, setting her glass of tea on the table very hard to add a little drama to her announcement.

"What? What do you need birth control for?" demanded Jake.

Roxie was enjoying his reaction, and said teasingly, "Well, I am a very popular girl, you know. And I'm very sexy—in case you hadn't noticed."

"Mom!" Jake sputtered. "Is she telling the truth?"

Michelle decided to play along with Roxie. "Well, you know, Jake, she really is pretty. I mean—better safe than sorry —don't you think?"

"Good grief!" said Jake, as Roxie giggled.

"Oh, she's putting you on, Jake. The pills are hormones to make her periods easier. I don't think she'll make the horse show this time, though. Too soon."

Jake was mollified. "*Sexy?* Who told you that, Roxie? So, are you going to take them?"

Michelle watched her—Roxie hadn't yet decided whether to take the drug, but she answered Jake's question: "No."

Michelle was surprised, but then she felt unaccountably proud of Roxie. She might change her mind later, of course, but now—not yet twelve years old—she'd thought about the drug with much more maturity than anyone might have expected from her.

She was tired, but it was good to be more relaxed with the kids than she'd been in a long time. "I thought I'd go to the mall after dinner. You guys want to go?"

* * *

About the same time that Michelle and the children left for the mall, Paul was paying the check for dinner at The Cove, Nana's favorite restaurant. He had expected her to be excited about their upcoming trip to Spain, but he'd been disappointed. In fact, he was more than disappointed; he'd counted on her excitement about the trip to distract her from noticing his reticence. He'd caught her looking at him over dinner with an odd expression on her face, and contrary to his expectation, she'd been more reticent than he was.

had not looked at her, but now his hand moved down
is eyes to cover his mouth and he looked at her with
. He couldn't speak. She rose then, crossed the space
them and cupped his chin in her frail hand. Her
re full of tenderness.

some sleep now, dear. It's almost three hours to the
ery. You should leave no later than seven, so don't
set your alarm."

* * *

had been trying to reach Paul on his cell for over two
He had finished the business he'd had in New York
uld fly back home on Tuesday afternoon instead of
sday. He'd made up his mind to buy the sports car
, and he was excited about it—he wanted to share the
th Paul. He intended to go straight to the dealer from
ort and buy the car. Michelle would raise hell, but
ldn't dare forbid Jake to have the car—not if Max had
given it to him.

As he helped her into the car, he wondered what he'd say
to her if she asked him what was wrong. The drive back to
her condo was almost ominously quiet, and his anxiety
quickened. He decided that as soon as they arrived, he
would say he was tired from the drive down from Atlanta
and wanted to go straight to bed, if she didn't mind. Actually,
he'd been looking forward to talking about the trip — the
hotel, the places they'd visit in the city. He'd been trying to
think of ways to locate her nieces and nephews; he hoped to
be able to surprise her by a visit with one or more of them, if
possible.

But she was so quiet, so serious, on the drive home, and
in the elevator up to her condo. In an unexpected turn of
events, it was he who asked her what was wrong when they
arrived in her sitting room; he'd been expecting her to ask
him that question.

She didn't answer, though. Instead, she sat down in her
chair by the balcony door and motioned for him to sit on the
little settee opposite her. "Sit down, dear," she said quietly.
The quietness was more commanding than mere politeness
would have been.

He sat, really concerned now. He could not remember
ever seeing Nana so serious. He'd been to the doctor's office
that afternoon, and he'd been given a positive report on her
condition. If anything new were wrong with her health, he
would have known about it from Dr. Hernandez. She was
clearly going to say something to him that she felt was
important, and it wasn't anything about her health. He waited
in silence.

She sighed deeply and then asked, "Paul, I prayed for Fr.
Murphy every day for many years. Why do you think I did
that?"

"Because you're a good Catholic, Nana." What was this
about? He didn't know she prayed for Father Murphy. "You
believe suicide is a mortal sin. I'm sure you prayed for his
soul."

"No. God knows things about us that we don't know ourselves. Father Murphy's suicide is between him and God." She looked at him with her eyes half-hooded and spoke quietly. "The pain that would drive anyone to so desperate a deed expiates much, I imagine. No, I didn't pray that he be forgiven for that sin." She looked at him for a moment in great tenderness, and then the moment was gone. Now her look was direct and full of firm resolve. "I prayed for him so that *I* could forgive him—because, no matter how justified it may be, anger is poisonous. It's like acid because it hurts its vessel much more than its object. The only way to overcome such wrath is to pray for the one who is its cause. I prayed for Father Murphy so that I could forgive him—for what he did to you."

Paul could feel the blood drain from his face, he could feel his hands grow cold—as though all the blood in his body were being withdrawn to his heart—to keep it working, to keep it alive. "I didn't know you knew...." he began, and stopped.

"I didn't—not at first. I was suspicious when you stopped serving at the altar, but I didn't know for sure. Then you went back to school, and not long after that, Father Murphy hanged himself." She turned her head a little to one side, as though she were deciding only then to tell him that she knew more. "But it's not what he did to you that concerns me now, Paul. I leave him to God. It's what *you* did to *him* that troubles me."

"What?"

"My prayer now is that *he* will forgive *you*."

Paul made several little movements on the settee. His hands on his knees, he started to stand, changed his mind, leaned back, then leaned forward and clasped his hands together with his elbows resting on his knees. "Nana, I—" he began. He wanted to say that he didn't understand, but he knew that was a lie. What he didn't understand was how she knew.

"I don't say that you seduced him, [...] what he did was anyone's fault but hi[...] talking now about what he did, but abo[...] did. You let him believe that the way y[...] You knew it wasn't—but you let him bel[...] believing that sin was on his soul. I pray[...] No, he is not my concern, Paul—*you* are.[...]

Paul lowered his head and turned his [...] He felt suddenly cold and his hands we[...] became so constricted he could hardly sp[...] you knew about that, Nana," he mumble[...]

"I understand, dear," she said gently.[...] then before she added pointedly, "It's n[...] understand what you did, but that *you* un[...]

He was too stunned to speak. For so[...] thought that he was protecting her from k[...] think she could bear, but all along, it had [...] protecting *him*—from a knowledge abou[...] didn't think *he* could bear. Worse—she [...] not recovered from the self-confrontation[...] that afternoon, and now this—*this*—comin[...] than he could handle. He put his hand acr[...]

"Now, listen, Paul," she continued. "I[...] much time I have, and I don't know how m[...] able to make sense." She wasn't smiling; sh[...] in some kind of charming self-mocker[...] speaking with the conciseness of serious in[...] do something for me, something I cannot d[...]

"Anything," he said in a whisper, his [...] tears.

"You must go and visit the Trappis[...] Lawrenceville tomorrow on your way back[...] know where it is. It's not out of your way. Y[...] Paul. You are not simply to say you will go. Y[...] have an appointment with a priest there tom[...] at ten o'clock. His name is Father Thomas.[...] you."

CHAPTER TWENTY-FIVE

The three hours' drive to Lawrenceville was a little dangerous because Paul had not slept. He'd set the alarm as Nana had suggested, but it was unnecessary. He was awake when the alarm sounded, and he lay there on the cool white sheets of her guestroom bed, his muscles stiff from lying in one position too long, and his mind blank. It hadn't been merely one of the worst nights in his life, but uniquely so. He'd been deprived of sleep at times in the past, by worry, fear, dread, and spent nights tossing and turning without rest, but that night he'd been still, even his mind was still—as though it were stunned—and he sensed that it wasn't over, that there was worse yet to come. He'd driven like a robot that morning; fortunately, there was little traffic to deal with.

Paul had been to the monastery once before when he was in his early teens on an acolytes' retreat from St. Rose's in Savannah almost twenty years ago. It was utterly unchanged, a cloistered compound set on several acres of woodland in the rolling piedmont south of Atlanta. The acolytes stayed in the retreat house, which was very austere—no television, no phones—and they followed a rigorous schedule: lights out at 8:00 p.m., rise before dawn for Mass. The setting of the monastery in rural woodland had the effect that untended nature always had on him—nature made Paul uncomfortable; all rural areas were strange, alien, to him. He'd always been much more at home in cities. The only place he'd been comfortable was the church. Just as he'd loved the stained-glass beauty of St. Rose's, he also liked the church at the monastery. It wasn't the vastness of the interior—after all, he was used to St. Patrick's in New York—it was its plainness. Trappists were committed to an ascetic life, sleeping in tiny

cells, eating plain food, spending every waking hour in labor
or prayer. The church's blank interior reflected the
asceticism that characterized their order. But in Paul's young,
developing artistic sense, the plainness had a kind of beauty
he'd found appealing.

He followed the winding driveway just past the church to
the retreat house. Besides single bedrooms, it held meeting
rooms, conference rooms, and small offices where members
of the public could go for confession or spiritual direction. A
receptionist greeted him. "Mr. Meyer? Father Thomas left a
message for you. Something came up—an emergency—and
he asked me to apologize to you. He'll be back right after
lunch. I'm sorry, sir. Maybe you'd like to rest, or perhaps
visit the church?"

Paul felt enormous relief. He'd been dreading the
appointment, almost holding his breath as he entered the
retreat house. "Oh, that's fine, just fine. I'll wander around, if
that's okay?"

She nodded. "Of course it is. There's a library on the
second floor—and of course, the church stays open all the
time. There's also a little chapel. It's new, just completed this
year. It's near the crypt." She stood up from her desk and
pointed through the window at her left. "You can see the
doorway just there—the Chapel of Our Lady of Guadalupe."

"Thanks," he said. "I think I can kill a couple of hours
without a problem."

"Oh, and lunch is served in the dining room just down
that hall at noon. Please feel free to join us. Of course, you
know, don't you, that meals are taken in silence?"

"Yes," he answered. "Actually, I've been here before,
many years ago." He turned to go up the stairs to the library,
but changed his mind and went outside to his car. He should
call Max. He'd already called Lolly to let her know that he
wouldn't be back until later today, maybe not until this
evening. He asked her to cancel two appointments for him
and notify Michelle that he'd be returning later than he

expected. Max had left voicemails, and Paul had put off returning his call as long as he dared. He didn't know how to explain to Max why he was here at the monastery. The universe had changed. He didn't even know how to say hello to him right now.

He started the car to turn on the air conditioning; the August heat was unbearable. Then he stared at his phone for several minutes before deciding that he'd just try to act as though everything were the same. It wasn't, but he didn't understand yet how it was different. He touched Max's number, got his voicemail, and left a message saying he'd try again later, so that Max wouldn't try to call him back. He put his forehead to the steering wheel and held it there, breathing a sigh of relief—reprieve, for now. He stayed there for at least ten minutes, feeling the blast of refrigerated air from the vents, his body and his mind too fatigued to think of what to do for the next hour and a half.

Finally he decided to visit the new chapel the receptionist mentioned and crossed the lawn to the crypt level of the church. It was cool and dark inside, a relief in itself, but he was also relieved to see the chapel's austerity. A picture of Our Lady of Guadalupe hung on the back wall, an unpleasant reminder of the night when he'd stumbled upon the Mexican cleaning woman saying prayers before a candle in the janitor's closet of the gallery, but otherwise, the chapel was blessedly unadorned. Thank God, he thought, there are no bleeding hearts in gilt frames, no weeping painted statues.

He sat down on one of the wooden straight chairs at the back of the chapel and made a conscious effort to empty his mind by looking at the bare walls. He had always known, in those moments when he was most honest with himself, that his only real love was beauty. His whole life had been about that love. He had no talent himself—he was no artist—but he had an "eye" for it, unlike most people. He was a procurer, a critic, a recognized authority. But now, sitting there in the dark bare room, Paul was hit with an unexpected realization:

It wasn't that he loved beauty. The truth was that he simply hated ugliness. His life had not really been about a love of beauty, but about that hate.

He leaned forward, putting his elbows on his knees and resting his chin in his hands. That startling realization had less impact than Nana's announcement the night before; it even had less impact than the admission he'd made to himself on the way to Savannah. Perhaps he'd been so fazed that he'd become somewhat numb. He sat there a long while, resting in the numbness, unaware of passing time. But then he glanced up at the picture of the Virgin.

What he first became aware of was predictable, a habit of mind: his first thoughts were *primitive realism*, and then, *masterpiece*. He thought that the real "miracle" about the legend surrounding the painting was how a primitive Mexican Indian peasant could have painted such a masterpiece centuries ago. The slight bowing toward the right of the Virgin's covered head above her folded hands was as perfect a *fiat* posture of obedience as any that might be imagined by the most sophisticated artist anywhere. It would have marked her unmistakably as the Blessed Virgin, even without the legend. He'd once seen the original, hanging in a basilica in Mexico City many years ago and thought it magnificent, though it was not regarded as art, but as a "miraculous" religious relic. He stared at the print, framed behind glass, and found the humility of the figure its single most compelling element—almost supernatural in effect.

But then, one part—and only one part—of the story of the picture came to mind: *She was pregnant.* He stared fixedly at the waistline below her hands, and his thoughts became less rational: She couldn't be pregnant—she was a painting. She was a painting made of some kind of canvas—probably not the stuff they said the fabric was made of, stuff that supposedly deteriorated rapidly, but ordinary cotton, maybe —and ordinary vegetable dyes made into paints at that time. There was a definite swell at that point in her waistline, but they had read it wrong. Pregnancy was unacceptable.

And finally, he realized that he was being irrational. *Why* was it unacceptable? Unacceptable to whom? To him. But why? What did it matter? Uncontrolled, formless nature outside the manmade chapel, the forest that surrounded the monastery, wilderness—that which is a force beyond human control—had invaded the chapel, invaded the painting, invaded her womb. He had to get out of there. As he opened the wooden door to leave the chapel, the intense light of an August day in Georgia almost blinded him. A bell chimed and he looked at his watch: It was noon and time for lunch— he realized he'd been sitting in the chapel more than an hour. "Oh, God," he whispered aloud, and nearly stumbled in the brightness toward the dining hall, grateful that it was time for lunch, that he had some kind of business-like destination at the moment, an errand, a task—*something* to take him legitimately away from where he was.

He joined a few other silent people—retreatants, likely—in the cafeteria-style dining room. It didn't seem odd that no one looked at anyone else, no one smiled a greeting. On the contrary, the silence was oddly polite, respectful. He realized he was hungry; the plain meal of meat loaf, green beans, and salad was indeed welcome. He ate staring ahead of him, his mind racing again. It occurred to him almost like an onset of panic that he had not once given thought to the coming appointment with Father Thomas. How should he approach this? Would the priest assume he was there for confession? Nana had made the appointment—how much had she told the priest?

The picture in the chapel loomed before his imagination —but the Virgin was transformed into Michelle, and in her womb was Roxie, and in Roxie's womb, another child—like one of those Russian dolls that come apart and hold another doll, and still another, representing continuity of life. Abstract and concrete, persons unknown and known, merged and blurred; he was crying. He shoved his dinner plate aside, wiped his cheeks with his fingers, and went to the little reception room to wait for Father Thomas.

CHAPTER TWENTY-SIX

He had to smile. The box of Kleenex on the small square table between two tattered armchairs revealed conclusively that the little room was indeed used for confession—called the "Sacrament of Reconciliation" by the Church.

Father Thomas sat in one of the chairs, smiling up at him. If Paul had any notion that the priest might look frighteningly "holy," he was disburdened of it right away. He was a homely little man, who, except for the monk's cowl, looked like any homely little nobody—a pock-marked face, apparently scarred from acne at an early age, eyeglasses—with thick and somewhat dirty lenses—in cheap, generic, black plastic frames, gray, grizzled crew-cut hair. Paul became immediately unguarded. This was an ordeal, but he'd just have to get through it and get back to Atlanta and to the gallery.

"Come in, Paul—Meyer, isn't it? I always forget that Estella's surname is Meyer—such a beautiful name, don't you think? It means "star." Puts me in mind of one of our Blessed Mother's titles, 'Star of the Sea.' How is she doing? Getting pretty old now, I imagine."

"She's doing well, Father, considering she's eighty now." He sat down opposite the priest and crossed an ankle over his knee, the expensive Italian leather loafer in stark contrast to the priest's bare, sandaled feet peeking from under the white cotton cowl. *Okay,* he thought, *little pleasantries done, what do we do now?* He put his arms on the arms of the chair and tried to keep his fingers from drumming.

Father Thomas rescued him. "You're here because your grandmother sent you."

"Yes. Yes, I am."

"Well, are you here to make confession?"

This was it. No wonder he hadn't thought about it, about what he'd say—because it was apparently *his* decision whether this would be an appointment for confession. "I—" he paused and took a deep breath. "I don't know, frankly. Nana made me promise to come here." He felt absurdly like a child being punished for some misbehavior or other.

"Yes, I see," answered Father Thomas. "Well, suppose you just start by telling me what this is all about, why she wanted you to come, okay? Then you can decide for yourself whether it's confession or not." His eyes, a watery-looking blue, were unnaturally large behind the thick lenses.

"Right. Okay. Well, to start, then—I'm gay." The large eyes behind the glasses didn't blink. He continued, "But this is about a priest—well, a priest and me."

"Oh," Father Thomas leaned forward. "Is this about an abuse?"

"Well, not exactly, to tell you the truth." Actually, he thought, it is. It's just that who abused whom might be questionable.

"How old were you?"

"Sixteen—almost seventeen."

Father Thomas took a Kleenex from the box and blew his nose loudly. "Excuse me," he said. "Allergies. Always have a problem this time of year." He dropped the tissue in a waste can by his chair. "Ah, yes. Seventeen. An acolyte, were you?"

Paul nodded. "Yes," the priest continued. "In close proximity, especially in the sacristy. Well, did he force himself on you?"

"No," Paul answered, shifting his weight a little in the chair.

"Right. They never do. They seduce you—statutory rape, in legal terms. Of course, it's evil in any terms."

The whole truth about the incident wasn't out yet, but Paul was beginning to relax. He felt good, in fact. It was the first time he'd ever told anyone anything about what happened, and the priest wasn't shocked—on the contrary. He seemed to be taking this almost casually. Paul began to

As he helped her into the car, he wondered what he'd say to her if she asked him what was wrong. The drive back to her condo was almost ominously quiet, and his anxiety quickened. He decided that as soon as they arrived, he would say he was tired from the drive down from Atlanta and wanted to go straight to bed, if she didn't mind. Actually, he'd been looking forward to talking about the trip — the hotel, the places they'd visit in the city. He'd been trying to think of ways to locate her nieces and nephews; he hoped to be able to surprise her by a visit with one or more of them, if possible.

But she was so quiet, so serious, on the drive home, and in the elevator up to her condo. In an unexpected turn of events, it was he who asked her what was wrong when they arrived in her sitting room; he'd been expecting her to ask him that question.

She didn't answer, though. Instead, she sat down in her chair by the balcony door and motioned for him to sit on the little settee opposite her. "Sit down, dear," she said quietly. The quietness was more commanding than mere politeness would have been.

He sat, really concerned now. He could not remember ever seeing Nana so serious. He'd been to the doctor's office that afternoon, and he'd been given a positive report on her condition. If anything new were wrong with her health, he would have known about it from Dr. Hernandez. She was clearly going to say something to him that she felt was important, and it wasn't anything about her health. He waited in silence.

She sighed deeply and then asked, "Paul, I prayed for Fr. Murphy every day for many years. Why do you think I did that?"

"Because you're a good Catholic, Nana." What was this about? He didn't know she prayed for Father Murphy. "You believe suicide is a mortal sin. I'm sure you prayed for his soul."

"No. God knows things about us that we don't know ourselves. Father Murphy's suicide is between him and God." She looked at him with her eyes half-hooded and spoke quietly. "The pain that would drive anyone to so desperate a deed expiates much, I imagine. No, I didn't pray that he be forgiven for that sin." She looked at him for a moment in great tenderness, and then the moment was gone. Now her look was direct and full of firm resolve. "I prayed for him so that *I* could forgive him—because, no matter how justified it may be, anger is poisonous. It's like acid because it hurts its vessel much more than its object. The only way to overcome such wrath is to pray for the one who is its cause. I prayed for Father Murphy so that I could forgive him—for what he did to you."

Paul could feel the blood drain from his face, he could feel his hands grow cold—as though all the blood in his body were being withdrawn to his heart—to keep it working, to keep it alive. "I didn't know you knew...." he began, and stopped.

"I didn't—not at first. I was suspicious when you stopped serving at the altar, but I didn't know for sure. Then you went back to school, and not long after that, Father Murphy hanged himself." She turned her head a little to one side, as though she were deciding only then to tell him that she knew more. "But it's not what he did to you that concerns me now, Paul. I leave him to God. It's what *you* did to *him* that troubles me."

"*What?*"

"My prayer now is that *he* will forgive *you.*"

Paul made several little movements on the settee. His hands on his knees, he started to stand, changed his mind, leaned back, then leaned forward and clasped his hands together with his elbows resting on his knees. "Nana, I—" he began. He wanted to say that he didn't understand, but he knew that was a lie. What he didn't understand was how she knew.

"I don't say that you seduced him, Paul. I don't say that what he did was anyone's fault but his own. But I'm not talking now about what he did, but about you and what you did. You let him believe that the way you live was his fault. You knew it wasn't—but you let him believe it was. He died believing that sin was on his soul. I pray he will forgive you. No, he is not my concern, Paul—*you* are."

Paul lowered his head and turned his face away from her. He felt suddenly cold and his hands were damp. His throat became so constricted he could hardly speak. "I didn't know you knew about that, Nana," he mumbled.

"I understand, dear," she said gently. A moment passed then before she added pointedly, "It's not important that I understand what you did, but that *you* understand it."

He was too stunned to speak. For so many years, he'd thought that he was protecting her from knowledge he didn't think she could bear, but all along, it had been *she* who was protecting *him*—from a knowledge about himself that she didn't think *he* could bear. Worse—she was right. He had not recovered from the self-confrontation he'd experienced that afternoon, and now this—*this*—coming now—was more than he could handle. He put his hand across his eyes.

"Now, listen, Paul," she continued. "I don't know how much time I have, and I don't know how much longer I'll be able to make sense." She wasn't smiling; she wasn't engaging in some kind of charming self-mockery. No, she was speaking with the conciseness of serious intent. "You must do something for me, something I cannot do myself."

"Anything," he said in a whisper, his eyes welling with tears.

"You must go and visit the Trappist monastery in Lawrenceville tomorrow on your way back to Atlanta. You know where it is. It's not out of your way. You must do this, Paul. You are not simply to say you will go. You will go. You have an appointment with a priest there tomorrow morning at ten o'clock. His name is Father Thomas. He's expecting you."

He had not looked at her, but now his hand moved down from his eyes to cover his mouth and he looked at her with anguish. He couldn't speak. She rose then, crossed the space between them and cupped his chin in her frail hand. Her eyes were full of tenderness.

"Get some sleep now, dear. It's almost three hours to the monastery. You should leave no later than seven, so don't forget to set your alarm."

* * *

Max had been trying to reach Paul on his cell for over two hours. He had finished the business he'd had in New York and could fly back home on Tuesday afternoon instead of Wednesday. He'd made up his mind to buy the sports car for Jake, and he was excited about it—he wanted to share the news with Paul. He intended to go straight to the dealer from the airport and buy the car. Michelle would raise hell, but she wouldn't dare forbid Jake to have the car—not if Max had already given it to him.

CHAPTER TWENTY-FIVE

The three hours' drive to Lawrenceville was a little dangerous because Paul had not slept. He'd set the alarm as Nana had suggested, but it was unnecessary. He was awake when the alarm sounded, and he lay there on the cool white sheets of her guestroom bed, his muscles stiff from lying in one position too long, and his mind blank. It hadn't been merely one of the worst nights in his life, but uniquely so. He'd been deprived of sleep at times in the past, by worry, fear, dread, and spent nights tossing and turning without rest, but that night he'd been still, even his mind was still—as though it were stunned—and he sensed that it wasn't over, that there was worse yet to come. He'd driven like a robot that morning; fortunately, there was little traffic to deal with.

Paul had been to the monastery once before when he was in his early teens on an acolytes' retreat from St. Rose's in Savannah almost twenty years ago. It was utterly unchanged, a cloistered compound set on several acres of woodland in the rolling piedmont south of Atlanta. The acolytes stayed in the retreat house, which was very austere—no television, no phones—and they followed a rigorous schedule: lights out at 8:00 p.m., rise before dawn for Mass. The setting of the monastery in rural woodland had the effect that untended nature always had on him—nature made Paul uncomfortable; all rural areas were strange, alien, to him. He'd always been much more at home in cities. The only place he'd been comfortable was the church. Just as he'd loved the stained-glass beauty of St. Rose's, he also liked the church at the monastery. It wasn't the vastness of the interior—after all, he was used to St. Patrick's in New York—it was its plainness. Trappists were committed to an ascetic life, sleeping in tiny cells, eating plain food, spending every waking hour in labor or prayer. The church's blank interior reflected the asceticism that characterized their order. But in Paul's young, developing artistic sense, the plainness had a kind of beauty he'd found appealing.

He followed the winding driveway just past the church to the retreat house. Besides single bedrooms, it held meeting rooms, conference rooms, and small offices where members of the public could go for confession or spiritual direction. A receptionist greeted him. "Mr. Meyer? Father Thomas left a message for you. Something came up—an emergency—and he asked me to apologize to you. He'll be back right after lunch. I'm sorry, sir. Maybe you'd like to rest, or perhaps visit the church?"

Paul felt enormous relief. He'd been dreading the appointment, almost holding his breath as he entered the retreat house. "Oh, that's fine, just fine. I'll wander around, if that's okay?"

She nodded. "Of course it is. There's a library on the second floor—and of course, the church stays open all the time. There's also a little chapel. It's new, just completed this year. It's near the crypt." She stood up from her desk and pointed through the window at her left. "You can see the doorway just there—the Chapel of Our Lady of Guadalupe."

"Thanks," he said. "I think I can kill a couple of hours without a problem."

"Oh, and lunch is served in the dining room just down that hall at noon. Please feel free to join us. Of course, you know, don't you, that meals are taken in silence?"

"Yes," he answered. "Actually, I've been here before, many years ago." He turned to go up the stairs to the library, but changed his mind and went outside to his car. He should call Max. He'd already called Lolly to let her know that he wouldn't be back until later today, maybe not until this evening. He asked her to cancel two appointments for him and notify Michelle that he'd be returning later than he expected. Max had left voicemails, and Paul had put off returning his call as long as he dared. He didn't know how to explain to Max why he was here at the monastery. The universe had changed. He didn't even know how to say hello to him right now.

He started the car to turn on the air conditioning; the August heat was unbearable. Then he stared at his phone for several minutes before deciding that he'd just try to act as though everything were the same. It wasn't, but he didn't understand yet how it was different. He touched Max's number, got his voicemail, and left a message saying he'd try again later, so that Max wouldn't try to call him back. He put his forehead to the steering wheel and held it there, breathing a sigh of relief—reprieve, for now. He stayed there for at least ten minutes, feeling the blast of refrigerated air from the vents, his body and his mind too fatigued to think of what to do for the next hour and a half.

Finally he decided to visit the new chapel the receptionist mentioned and crossed the lawn to the crypt level of the church. It was cool and dark inside, a relief in itself, but he was also relieved to see the chapel's austerity. A picture of Our Lady of Guadalupe hung on the back wall, an unpleasant reminder of the night when he'd stumbled upon the Mexican cleaning woman saying prayers before a candle in the janitor's closet of the gallery, but otherwise, the chapel was blessedly unadorned. Thank God, he thought, there are no bleeding hearts in gilt frames, no weeping painted statues.

He sat down on one of the wooden straight chairs at the back of the chapel and made a conscious effort to empty his mind by looking at the bare walls. He had always known, in those moments when he was most honest with himself, that his only real love was beauty. His whole life had been about that love. He had no talent himself—he was no artist—but he had an "eye" for it, unlike most people. He was a procurer, a critic, a recognized authority. But now, sitting there in the dark bare room, Paul was hit with an unexpected realization:

It wasn't that he loved beauty. The truth was that he simply hated ugliness. His life had not really been about a love of beauty, but about that hate.

He leaned forward, putting his elbows on his knees and resting his chin in his hands. That startling realization had less impact than Nana's announcement the night before; it even had less impact than the admission he'd made to himself on the way to Savannah. Perhaps he'd been so fazed that he'd become somewhat numb. He sat there a long while, resting in the numbness, unaware of passing time. But then he glanced up at the picture of the Virgin.

What he first became aware of was predictable, a habit of mind: his first thoughts were *primitive realism*, and then, *masterpiece*. He thought that the real "miracle" about the legend surrounding the painting was how a primitive Mexican Indian peasant could have painted such a masterpiece centuries ago. The slight bowing toward the right of the Virgin's covered head above her folded hands was as perfect a *fiat* posture of obedience as any that might be imagined by the most sophisticated artist anywhere. It would have marked her unmistakably as the Blessed Virgin, even without the legend. He'd once seen the original, hanging in a basilica in Mexico City many years ago and thought it magnificent, though it was not regarded as art, but as a "miraculous" religious relic. He stared at the print, framed behind glass, and found the humility of the figure its single most compelling element—almost supernatural in effect.

But then, one part—and only one part—of the story of the picture came to mind: *She was pregnant.* He stared fixedly at the waistline below her hands, and his thoughts became less rational: She couldn't be pregnant—she was a painting. She was a painting made of some kind of canvas—probably not the stuff they said the fabric was made of, stuff that supposedly deteriorated rapidly, but ordinary cotton, maybe —and ordinary vegetable dyes made into paints at that time. There was a definite swell at that point in her waistline, but they had read it wrong. Pregnancy was unacceptable.

And finally, he realized that he was being irrational. *Why* was it unacceptable? Unacceptable to whom? To him. But why? What did it matter? Uncontrolled, formless nature outside the manmade chapel, the forest that surrounded the monastery, wilderness—that which is a force beyond human control—had invaded the chapel, invaded the painting, invaded her womb. He had to get out of there. As he opened the wooden door to leave the chapel, the intense light of an August day in Georgia almost blinded him. A bell chimed and he looked at his watch: It was noon and time for lunch— he realized he'd been sitting in the chapel more than an hour. "Oh, God," he whispered aloud, and nearly stumbled in the brightness toward the dining hall, grateful that it was time for lunch, that he had some kind of business-like destination at the moment, an errand, a task—*something* to take him legitimately away from where he was.

He joined a few other silent people—retreatants, likely—in the cafeteria-style dining room. It didn't seem odd that no one looked at anyone else, no one smiled a greeting. On the contrary, the silence was oddly polite, respectful. He realized he was hungry; the plain meal of meat loaf, green beans, and salad was indeed welcome. He ate staring ahead of him, his mind racing again. It occurred to him almost like an onset of panic that he had not once given thought to the coming appointment with Father Thomas. How should he approach this? Would the priest assume he was there for confession? Nana had made the appointment—how much had she told the priest?

The picture in the chapel loomed before his imagination —but the Virgin was transformed into Michelle, and in her womb was Roxie, and in Roxie's womb, another child—like one of those Russian dolls that come apart and hold another doll, and still another, representing continuity of life. Abstract and concrete, persons unknown and known, merged and blurred; he was crying. He shoved his dinner plate aside, wiped his cheeks with his fingers, and went to the little reception room to wait for Father Thomas.

feel a burden lift from him, a burden he'd apparently become so accustomed to that he'd forgotten it was there. But he hadn't yet told the whole truth of the matter.

"Father," he said, "I have to be honest about this. The priest did not seduce me—not exactly anyway."

Father Thomas raised his eyebrows, took a tissue and blew his nose again, then leaned back in his chair. "Maybe you should just tell me what happened."

So Paul told him—everything. He knew he was gay before it happened, he said, but then he changed it: "No, I don't mean 'before it happened'; I mean—" He stopped and cleared his throat. "I mean before I *did* it." A knot rose in his throat then, so hard and so tight, he thought he would strangle.

He looked down at himself, avoiding the priest's face, but he could hear him ask quietly, "Why did you do it?"

"Because he was ugly!"

A dam rose to bursting point. A single, great, dry sob wrenched itself from his throat. There were no tears. He raised his eyes to the priest and wiped his hand across his mouth. "Because he was ugly," he repeated, as though he wanted to hear it himself instead of the priest in the chair across from him.

Father Thomas leaned back and looked at him dispassionately. There was no judgment in his face, not even curiosity. Rather, he simply looked like someone who was settling in to read a book, watch a film or hear a tale. "Continue," he said, "if you want to."

"I do. I want to very much," Paul answered. He had to now. A thick, dark fog was clearing, and he had to see what it was hiding. "Sex," he said simply, and stopped. He began again, "Sex...can be hate." Father Thomas nodded. "It can be anger," Paul continued, "even rage, maybe, an intent to harm, to punish."

Even before the priest asked, Paul knew the answer.

"Who did you hate, Paul? With whom were you so angry?"

"My father," he said. "But you knew that, didn't you." It was a statement.

"Of course," Father Thomas replied. "We only hate those we love."

And it was that simple remark that broke the dam. For the next three hours, Paul wept and talked. He and Father Thomas together went through the box of Kleenex and another had to be located in a cabinet behind the priest's chair. Paul talked about his family, about his grandmother, his parents, his childhood, even about art. He talked about *everything*. He talked excitedly sometimes—about his planned vacation with Nana in Barcelona and his hope that she'd be homesick for Savannah. He even talked about Max, and about the conflict he was experiencing over Max's family, but only the surface conflict where adultery entered the picture; he didn't go into the strange depths he'd experienced on the drive down to Savannah. He didn't know how to express that part. It wasn't clear in his own mind, so that when it approached the surface, he stumbled over it, inarticulate. He talked about his work at the gallery, even about Jake's raw talent. By the time he finished, he had even talked about the rural areas on the interstate, wondering why he didn't like driving through them—though he was beginning to detect another fog there, and he stopped.

"My God, Father," he said, empty for now, and looking at his watch. "It's 4:00. I hope I haven't kept you from anything important."

"No, no. This is important. Do you want to drive on to Atlanta now? Would you like a cup of tea first?" He had not asked Paul whether he wanted to make a confession. He stood and looked out the window. "Hey, look outside. It's pouring. Let's have tea before you leave. Maybe the rain will pass."

But there was something else, and it had to be said. "Father, the priest I told you about? He committed suicide. That's why Nana made me come here."

"Oh." Father Thomas sat down again. His pocked face

became sorrowful. "Do you want to make confession now, Paul?"

* * *

When Lolly told Michelle that morning that Paul wouldn't return until late, her first reaction was irritation, but then she felt guilty about that. Paul wouldn't leave her to run the gallery alone unless something was wrong—probably something to do with his grandmother. She wanted to call him then, to ask if everything was all right, but if something really was wrong, her call would only be an interruption, so she decided against it.

He called her at home that night. Max had returned a day early, and they were having dinner at the time. Paul's voice sounded very tight and strange. He said he'd be back in the morning and apologized for being late in returning. He didn't mention his grandmother, or say anything about what was wrong.

CHAPTER TWENTY-SEVEN

Max was tying his tie in the mirror; Michelle was rummaging through her closet about ten feet away from him. He asked her whether Paul had said what time he'd be back today.

"No. I told you—he just said he'd be back this morning, sometime before lunch. Why?"

"Just wondered." He dropped the subject. He'd been very disappointed when he got back to Atlanta and Paul wasn't there; he had wanted Paul to go with him to buy Jake's car. Buying it had lost the joy he'd anticipated because Paul wasn't there. The car and Paul were somehow connected for him. As it turned out, he'd just put a deposit on the car to hold it. Some sense of reason had interrupted the fun: Jake might not like it—as hard as that was to imagine.

"I hope nothing is seriously wrong with his grandmother," Michelle continued.

"Probably not. No telling what he ran into trying to get her ready for the trip to Spain."

"Well, I'm just glad he's coming back this morning. I've had a hell of a time." She was pulling on a black skirt, a Jourdano design with an uneven hemline, and she thought it was tacky—too trendy. This would be the last time she'd wear it. "I'm taking that picture of Roxie that Jake did to the gallery. I want to ask Paul if there isn't some way it can be entered in the young artists' competition. But since Jake's the son of a Hunter employee, I figured Paul would automatically say 'no.' So, I thought—if he's looking at it at the time—it's downright fantastic—maybe we can come up with something somehow, maybe through one of the groups holding the separate competitions."

"Good luck with that. He won't agree to it." It occurred to Max that if the picture couldn't be entered, Jake might not care so much, not while he was driving his chrome yellow Nissan GT-R.

* * *

It was still raining yesterday evening after Paul's confession, and Father Thomas suggested that Paul stay in the retreat house overnight and drive back in the morning, especially since he'd had no sleep the night before. Paul had poured out all his confusion about Max in a jumble of words that didn't even make sense to him; it probably wouldn't have made sense to anyone except the little priest. *Michelle, kids, abstract and concrete, known persons and unknown.* And even *Russian doll.* It wasn't hard for Father Thomas to put it together.

"Don't tell me to 'pray' about it, Father," said Paul. "I can't do that. I don't think I really believe, and there's a limit to hypocrisy even for me. But I've broken my mind about it by asking over and over and over, *What should I do?*"

"Well, maybe you don't know it, but that's praying. And don't tell me there wasn't an answer. There's *always* an answer."

"There was...something. But it was not an answer."

"Describe it," the priest encouraged him.

"It wasn't a voice, not even a sound, really—more like a resonance—all I got, over and over, was 'Love.'" He stopped, as if remembering, then blurted out angrily, "*But that's not an answer!* Good grief, *that* is the problem. I needed a solution—I *know* what the problem is!"

"You're wrong," the priest said. "That *was* the answer."

Paul raised his eyes to the priest's pock-marked face, to his dirty black-framed eyeglasses—none of which he saw now. Father Thomas blew his nose again and said, "You know that love is the only thing that really matters to any of us.

Everybody knows that—*everybody*. That's not some big secret we have to 'discover.'"

"I love him. I love him more than anything in the world."

"I know you do—I mean, I know how you feel. But you're not loving him just because of what you feel. You asked what you should do—and you got your answer. But you can't do it. Because you don't know how. And *that* is what's causing your pain—not love." He looked at Paul's haggard face, then said, "You can't do this. Go out to the reception desk and tell Meg to give you a room. The best thing you can do right now is get some sleep. I'm going to leave a name and phone number with her—somebody in Atlanta who may be able to help you."

But as he left the retreat house the next morning, he shoved the little piece of paper into his pocket and forgot about it. His mind was clear for the moment, as though it had been purged, and he drove back to Atlanta thinking only of what lay ahead at the gallery. After he called Michelle last night, he called Nana. He knew she'd be waiting to hear from him. The conversation had been brief.

"Are you all right, darling?" she asked.

"Yes, Nana. I'm okay. And thank you, dear." That was all he wanted to say about Father Thomas. He'd had an emotional catharsis, and no matter what else may or may not have come of his encounter with the little priest, that much had been profoundly good for him.

She asked for no details. "Well, listen, dear," she answered. "I wanted to mention it to you when you came— you should cancel the hotel in Barcelona right away. There's probably a deadline for cancellation. I've been in touch with Juana, my sister's granddaughter, and she's said we should stay with her."

Was there no end to her surprises? He'd been trying to think of a way to locate one of her relatives; she'd done it on her own. "How did you find her?"

"I just wrote to my sister's old address. She's been dead

for years, but Juana said the letter was forwarded to her
mother—she lives in Majorca now—and her mother sent the
letter to her in Barcelona. It took a while, but she got it, and
she called me last week."

He didn't call Max. It was 7:30 by the time he called
Nana, and he knew Max wouldn't be expecting him to call at
that hour; he'd be at home by then.

The apartment looked strange to him when he arrived
that Wednesday morning. He'd been away only two nights
but it felt as though he'd been gone for a month. He
showered and changed. Putting his dirty clothes in the
laundry basket, he found in his pocket the yellow sticky note
that Father Thomas left for him with the number for a
Father Walter Bazenski. Yes, he would call when he got to
the office.

* * *

Lolly buzzed Michelle to tell her that Paul was back, and
she took a sheet of notepaper with her into his office—
questions she needed to ask, information he needed to have.
She also took the portfolio with Jake's picture of Roxie.

"Wow, you were missed!" She leaned the portfolio
against the wall.

"Yeah, well, I'm sorry I didn't get back yesterday."

"That's okay. We survived. I've got some stuff here to go
over with you, but first, let me ask you: Can we get Jake's
picture in the competition somehow?" She took the picture
out and propped it against the portfolio on the floor.

Paul looked at it. It *was* so impressive. But he smiled at
her: "You know better than that."

"Yes, I do, but I thought maybe if it came through one of
the groups— "

"Sure—a group he's been a member of for years, right?"
He grinned at her. "Sorry, love. Look, you said it yourself: if
he's into it, it'll work out. He doesn't need to win any
contest."

"I know, I know." She returned the smile and started to put the picture away.

"No, leave it there, please. I want to enjoy it for a while."

He made some calls after she left. First, he cancelled the hotel reservation in Spain. Then he started to call Max, but he called the number Father Thomas had left him instead.

A gruff voice answered, "Father Bazenski here."

Paul told him that Father Thomas at the monastery had given him the name and number. "He said he thought you might be able to help me with...to help me with a certain situation I have."

"Okay. Well, let me see. I've got some time this afternoon around four."

Paul met Max every Wednesday at four o'clock at Gino's. He made a decision. "I can be there. Where are you?"

"St. Andrew's. Do you know where that is? It's on Eighth Avenue."

Paul knew. It was a slummy part of the city, but he'd be there. After he hung up, he called Max.

"Damn, Paul! I've been waiting to hear from you. Is your grandmother okay?"

"Yes, she's fine. Sorry I couldn't call sooner."

"Well, guess what. I bought the car—I mean, I made a deposit to hold it, anyway. I wanted you with me so bad. Jake's going to love it. Do you think you could be with me when I give it to him? No—no, that's not a good idea."

Paul heard his voice deflate as he realized that impossibility. *Poor Max.* "Well, listen," Paul said, not pursuing the subject. "I can't be at Gino's this afternoon. I've got an appointment." *Deception spreads*, he thought, *once it's chosen.*

Max wanted to go to the apartment that night, but Paul said no—too much work to do to catch up. He'd call him tomorrow.

CHAPTER TWENTY-EIGHT

At four that afternoon, Paul pulled the door of St. Andrew's open. The church was old, dark red brick, soot-stained from the factories that used to litter the area, now standing empty and derelict with broken windows. He worried about his car parked by the curb in front the church, hoping the Mercedes hubcaps would still be there when he returned.

Double doors to an office in bright fluorescent light stood open to the left of the vestibule where he stood, and he crossed the cracked tile floor to enter there. A young African-American woman sat behind the desk, her head covered in multiple small braids with colored beads, and her long nails painted in multiple colors, each with a different design.

"Can I help you?" She looked up at him from the most perfectly round eyes he'd ever seen, their roundness accentuated by their enormous size.

"I have an appointment with Father Bazenski. My name is Paul Meyer."

"Yes, sir. Go on in and have a seat. He'll be here pretty soon."

He went into the priest's office and sat down in a blue vinyl chair opposite the priest's littered desk. In a moment Father Bazenski came in, wearing a tee-shirt and jeans. He looked to be about fifty; his hair was thinning on top, and he had a few lines in his face.

"Hi, Paul. Sorry to keep you waiting. We're trying to clean out some stuff in the thrift store down in the basement." He closed the door behind him.

"That's okay. I just got here."

"It's not a 'nice' neighborhood, I know. But don't worry

about your car. Nobody around here ever bothers a car parked in front of the church—not even a Mercedes." He smiled at Paul and sat down behind his desk. "Father Thomas sent you. Right. So, are you 'gay'?"

"Well," said Paul, taken aback. "That's pretty blunt."

"The only people Thomas ever refers to me say they're 'gay.' Sorry about that. I'm the Courage chaplain here. Do you know what that is?"

"Never heard of it."

"Well, I'll tell you about it in a minute. Let's talk a little bit first. Would you call yourself a 'homosexual,' Paul? That's what you mean by 'gay,' right?"

"Yes. Yes, I would." He was immediately uncomfortable. Were they going to play silly word games? He wanted to leave already.

As if he could read his thoughts, Father Bazenski said, "You're not going to enjoy the next minute or two. I apologize for that in advance. I'm not engaging in some kind of semantic argument, but there's no such thing as 'a homosexual.' It's a word that describes a certain type of activity. You can't *be* an activity. You are a person who acts; you're not that activity. All God's creatures are sexual—even me. Sex—any kind — is what we do, it's not what we *are*. A lot of people—both 'gay' and 'straight'—have been telling you otherwise. They've been telling you that you 'can't help yourself,' but that's not true. Of course you can."

"Father, I appreciate what you're trying to do—really, I do. But I've been gay all my life. It's not a choice, and it's not something you can 'cure' as though it were some kind of illness or disease. It's the way I *am*. It's *what* I am. I can't help that. I can't change what I am. See, what you're saying may be appropriate for someone who doesn't accept the fact that they're gay—but I do. It's what I am and I acknowledge and accept it. Self-acceptance is everything."

"But it's *not* what you 'are;' it's what you 'do.' And you've got to get hold of that. It's critical."

"Why? That's just word games. It doesn't make any difference."

"Oh, yes it does. To say that you do what you do because of what you 'are' says that you can't control your actions. People who can't control their sexual actions? Get serious. We lock people like that up."

"Okay. It's what I'm attracted to that I can't help—or since we're being so precise, *to whom* I'm attracted—better grammar."

"Right. You are a man who has an attraction to other men. Right?"

"Yes," Paul answered slowly. Where was this going? He could feel anger swelling in him like a threatening wave, not because he believed the priest was wrong, but because he was offended—by someone who could have no idea of what it meant to be gay. But more than that, Paul was offended by the priest's lack of caution—his apparent lack of fear that he might offend. He seemed not even to care whether he was offending Paul or not.

"Look, if you say that your sexual appetite controls your actions, you're saying that you're no different from my dog Duke. He can't control his sexual appetite either. Gets him in trouble all the time. But you're not a dog. *You* can make choices—Duke can't."

"I can't make myself attracted to women," Paul argued.

"Maybe not. But you make choices about your behavior. *Sane* people do. I repeat, we lock the others up. They *can't* make choices. It's a matter of being versus doing. But the point is, to define yourself *as* what you do is to disclaim any responsibility for it."

For a long moment, Father Bazenski's words hung in the air between them. Paul could not answer. Despite his fatigue, he wanted almost desperately to answer—even to stand up, walk around the desk and hit the priest squarely in the face. But he did nothing, said nothing—because the man had not said anything Paul could honestly disagree with.

How could he answer him? What was there to say in his
own defense? And why did he feel any need to defend
himself? Against what? Against the suggestion that he could
make choices about his own behavior?

His mind riffled through his memory like flipping pages
backward: When had he made conscious decisions about
sex and what were the grounds of those decisions? Only his
own desire, or the possibility of rejection or acceptance,
other practical, self-serving matters. Mayfield, for example.
He was very attracted to the artist, but he'd decided not to
follow through with it after the last encounter—because
Mayfield wanted to form an attachment, and Paul didn't.
There'd been other times he chose not to follow his
attraction, his desire. But he'd never tried to deny the desire
itself. Why? Because it never occurred to him that he
should, it never occurred to him that he *could.* He'd just
chosen not to follow through sometimes. So—if he wasn't
angry by the idea that he could choose, what was he angry
about?

"Listen," Father Bazenski leaned forward. "You are a
person, a human being. And unlike Duke, you're given the
dignity—and the burden—of choice, of what we call 'free will.'
And a person chooses what he does; he is not *himself* what
he chooses. You eat dinner—you are not dinner, no matter
what kind of dinner you eat. You have sex—you're not sex,
no matter what kind it is. Now." He looked at Paul very
directly. "Say that is true," he said. His voice was very quiet,
but insistent. "Say it."

Paul felt assaulted. He'd never felt so offended in his life
—yet there was nothing in what the priest said to argue with.
What he said was simple and obviously true—then why was
he so profoundly offended by the words? He told himself
that it was because the priest insisted he say them. Whatever
the reason, he found it almost impossible to get the words
out—but he had to say them because he had to get out of
there. "That—is—true." Why was that so hard? And why did
it make him so angry?

"Good!" said the priest. "*Courage* is the name of a group of men who meet here at St. Andrew's—a small group, never more than a dozen or so—in the basement next to the thrift shop every Thursday night at 7:30. They are men who deal with same-sex attraction, men just like you. No different from you, and no different from other men except that they contend with a kind of desire they do not want. If you decide that you also have desires you don't want, you're welcome to join us—if you want to. I'm inviting you to join us tomorrow night, but you don't have to answer right now. In fact, I'd rather you didn't. Think about it. Okay?" He stood up.

Paul stood as well and shook the priest's hand. "Thanks, I'll think about it." He was just being polite; he had no intention of going to the meeting. But when he reached the door, he turned around before opening it. "Why did you make me say 'that is true'—being versus doing?"

"Because it's not enough just to agree with it, and certainly not enough just to refrain from arguing with it—because it makes you too mad to argue. You have to *know it's true.* Otherwise, you're lost. You drown in what people tell you about yourself, even though they mean well. But if you believe them, it makes you give up your freedom. You abandon yourself, your own dignity and your humanity. You just surrender to whatever forces pull you under, and you let those forces define you. Knowing that you can make choices about what you do is your life jacket. If you deny that, if you choose to believe you 'can't help yourself,' then you can't help yourself. *Courage* is deep water, be warned. But everybody there has a life jacket. If you didn't have one, I wouldn't invite you—I wouldn't let you come at all."

The hubcaps were still on the car. It hadn't been dented or keyed. He drove home.

CHAPTER TWENTY-NINE

Max was having some difficulty accepting Paul's excuse of "too much work," even though he knew it could well be true. They'd both been away, and so he'd looked forward especially to their standing Wednesday date at Gino's. Paul's breaking of that date seemed ominous to Max, even if the excuse was a valid one. Before Paul left for Savannah, when Max had made that terrible *faux pas* of suggesting a separation from his family, Paul's reaction frightened him. And he hadn't forgotten it. His real difficulty in accepting Paul's excuse had its source in Max's desire to grasp at that which he most feared losing: Paul's love. The idea that he might lose Paul by his own mistake only increased his insecurity.

He felt a sense of urgency that was quite apart from his desire to see him. Sitting at his desk on Thursday morning, frowning, not attending to the work that needed his attention, he decided to call Paul, suggest lunch, and then at lunch, he would suggest dinner at DeJong's and a trip back to the apartment. He could have a "dinner appointment with a client;" Michelle never questioned such appointments. Unlike Max, Paul never had to worry about appeasing other people, deceiving them, he thought grimly—then reminded himself that Paul had to work with Michelle every day, and with both chagrin and relief, he decided the burden was equal. What was wrong, and what was needed to repair the wrong, was as simple as it was difficult: divorce. But he dared not bring it up again.

* * *

Max didn't know—couldn't know—that for Paul, it was no longer that simple. The bitterness of his experience on the road to Savannah, Nana's revelation, and last but far from least, his marathon conference with Father Thomas had complicated the situation in ways that Max wouldn't have understood even if he'd known. Paul was acutely aware of the adultery he and Max committed, but it was more than that now. The "known and unknown" behind that simple adultery was becoming heavier to bear by the minute, or so it seemed to him, as it crept unbidden around the edges of his thought. Michelle and the children were known to Paul, and loved by him, but that very love had unlocked a door that he might well wish he'd left securely shut, a door through which "unknowns" entered—in vast numbers, and over space and time far greater than merely the here and now. Though he couldn't understand—nor did he try—it seemed to Paul now that he, Max, and any problems, any kind of difficulties they had at all, were receding, and losing significance. Ironically, though for very different reasons, he was as grasping and insecure as Max, so when Max called him for lunch, he didn't hesitate.

At Lombardi's, Max was waiting for him at noon, sitting where he could see Paul enter, and when he did, Max's face lit up like a child's face seeing Santa Claus at Christmas. It was difficult for both of them to keep from touching hands when Paul sat down at the table.

"God, it's good to see you," whispered Max.

Paul smiled. Indeed it was good to see Max, too. He felt as though he'd been gone away a very long time, not just a few days. He wanted so much just to reach across the table to touch him, even though he realized that it was the impossibility of touching that made the desire so intense. Would that desire be so great if two men holding hands across a restaurant table were normal?

"Is everything okay with your grandmother? I mean, you had to stay an extra day—I've been wondering if she's all right."

"Oh, yes, she's fine. I just had some trouble getting in to see her doctor. He had to squeeze me in between appointments." He departed from their habit then of never mentioning Michelle: "But, you know, Michelle did very well without me—even made a ten-thousand dollar sale."

"Yeah. She's better at that kind of thing than she thinks she is," said Max, and changed the subject. "Jake's car is sitting at the dealer's waiting for the great surprise. I don't know if I can wait for his birthday. I wish you could be with us."

"Well, I was going to ask you—what about Michelle and the car? Did she finally agree to this? If she did, you didn't say so."

"No. Look, dammit, I just decided I'm not going to let Jake lose this car because she's paranoid. It's not going to happen. Just not fair to him."

"To him? Or to you?" Paul was smiling, teasing him, but he added, "I'm not sure that I don't agree with his mother. Seems dangerous—a high-powered sports car for a kid that age—kind of reckless."

"Bullshit. Jake's mature for his age. Anyway, I haven't bought it yet." He didn't really want to talk about the car; he didn't really want to talk at all: "I'm having a hard time focusing on anything. I want to be alone with you right now." Paul smiled and raised his brows to imply that he felt the same. "Listen," Max continued. "I was going to suggest dinner at DeJong's tonight and a trip back to the apartment —but let's skip dinner, okay?"

"Can't." replied Paul. "Got a dinner appointment with a Hunter patron."

* * *

Paul had no dinner appointment. He went back to the gallery after lunch wondering why he'd told Max that he did. He had no intention of going to Father Bazenski's Courage group, but he must have wanted to keep the option open. By mid-afternoon, his confusion about his own intentions reached a point where a decision had to be made. He had enough work to do at the office to keep him there until at least 6:00; then he'd get a quick dinner and drop in on the meeting—he was invited, after all, and if he didn't like it, he could always leave. Nothing lost—except a chance to be with Max.

As it turned out, Paul arrived late—almost 8:30. It wasn't quite dark yet, but he felt glad to see the single light shining above a door to what was obviously the basement, next to the wide concrete steps he'd ascended yesterday afternoon. The neighborhood, with its shut storefronts, made him nervous. He entered a dark hall and saw a lighted open doorway toward the end, from which voices and laughter came.

Father Bazenski looked up when he came in. "Come in, Paul. I didn't think you were coming. Afraid you missed the meeting. Everybody just left a few minutes ago, but we're staying a little while for some coffee."

Paul smiled. "Sorry I'm late. Had a lot of work to catch up on." Actually, he'd dawdled over what was supposed to be a quick dinner, apparently still unsure that he'd go to the meeting until he'd already arrived. He was glad now that he'd arrived too late for the meeting itself, but he was aware that his escape was covered by a lie.

One of the men, a nearly bald, portly middle-aged man, motioned to an empty chair. Other than the priest, there were four other men present—one of them Paul recognized, a strikingly handsome young man who was, if Paul remembered correctly, a model. He'd met him at a couple of gay social events a year ago, but he couldn't remember his name. The young man recognized Paul, stood and shook his hand. "I think I've met you," he said. "My name's Steven."

"Paul. Yes, I think we met at Joe Lumpkin's party—what was it? A year ago?" He sat down and glanced at the other two men: a business suit and glasses, about forty, and a nervous-looking kid, maybe twenty, with spiked hair and some kind rock band tee-shirt.

Father Bazenski was hospitable. "There's still some coffee left over there on the counter if you like." He motioned toward a coffeepot and stacked Styrofoam cups. "Almost everybody was here for the meeting. Two of our group are on vacation—Ed took his family down to Disney World—and where did Jesse go?" He looked around at the others for an answer.

The portly man said, "Upstate New York—visiting his parents."

"Oh, right, yes. Well, let's introduce ourselves to Paul. He knows you already, Steve." He turned to Paul, "We don't use last names here." Then he nodded toward the business suit.

"Malcolm. I'm a doctor."

The nervous-looking kid said, "Johnny. Musician."

The portly man said, "Father Bernie. Priest."

Father Murphy instantly sprang to Paul's mind: *Too bad there was no group called Courage there for him. I wish there had been—for both our sakes.* He didn't feel at all uncomfortable—at least, not yet—and so he kept an open mind about the group. But at the same time, he felt self-conscious and more than a little defensive. Was he expected to give some kind of "testimony"—like they do in AA meetings? That was not going to happen, he decided.

Father Bazenski had some pages stapled together; he was flipping some of the pages forward. "I was just telling everybody about this report, Paul. Kind of interesting analysis of the causes of same-sex attraction. Just a brief recap for you since you missed the meeting: There are a few rare cases of hormonal imbalances that result in SSA, but generally, statistics reveal almost universal trouble with the same-sex parent."

Paul was interested. "Oh? So, that's proven, is it?"

The doctor answered, "Well, no, there's no way to prove

a causal relationship, but the stats are too strong to be dismissed. Certainly have to say they're interesting."

The group talked for a while about the report. Paul remained quiet and listened. Finally, Father Bazenski said, "It helps to know this information only insofar as it always helps to understand oneself in a bigger picture. Nothing more. An unacknowledged basic need can easily become eroticized. Reminds me of a woman I used to know. Intelligent, attractive, but compulsive abusive relationships with men. She spent two expensive years with a shrink before she found out she was still looking for her father's love— he'd abandoned her when she was a small child. She was so happy to find out the cause of her chronic self-destructive behavior—trouble is, knowing what caused it didn't change it. I don't know if she ever changed it. Knowing causes of whatever doesn't really help much."

Paul thought of his father, of Max's father, but the thought of Max brought a sudden wave of sadness, of longing, and then, guilt. He felt he was being *unfaithful* to his beloved; the lie about having dinner with a patron suddenly seemed cruel, brutal even—and *wrong*, in every way.

And while he was thinking of Max, the spike-haired kid, Johnny, turned to him and said, "Something else that helps is to try to put your difficulty in words. Have you done that, Paul?"

Paul took a deep breath. Was this it? If it was, he wasn't ready for it. He felt desperately self-protective, but he didn't know the feeling for what it was. In his belief, it was Max he was protecting, not himself. "My *difficulty*," he said, saying the word in a mocking tone that was conspicuously unnecessary, "is that I love someone, someone who is not of the right gender." One eyebrow lifted to reinforce his self-conscious sarcasm.

Father Bazenski smiled a little sadly. The others dropped their eyes and didn't look at him, as though they were embarrassed for him. He was aware suddenly that he'd been wrong—the spike-haired kid had not been asking him for some kind of "testimony." But realizing his own mistake only made him angrier. The other priest—Bernie—looked at him with an expression of gentleness that made Paul angry: as though he were a little boy who'd knocked a baseball through a window and broken it, and was now claiming he didn't do it, protesting that he was innocent. And Paul felt like that little boy, he felt defensive and angry. What had he expected in response to his claim of "love"? Sympathy? Murmurs of understanding? But the room was simply silent. No one looked at him. He didn't know what to do, what to say.

Finally, Father Bazenski spoke. His voice was kind but firm. "Why don't you spend some time thinking about your 'difficulty,' Paul. Then we can talk about it next week—if you want to."

It seemed he had no alternative. No one was talking, no one even looked at him. Humiliated, he pushed his chair back, stood up without looking at them, and left the room, feeling like a child sent from the classroom for bad behavior. He drove home with tears crowding the edge of his vision, and when he got to his apartment, he found the door unlocked. Max was there! Max had a key!

And there he was. Sitting on the sofa, eating popcorn, and watching a movie. He looked up at Paul uncertainly: "I decided to surprise you...hope you don't mind."

"*Mind?* Oh, God, Max!" He fell on the sofa next to him, wanting with all his heart never to be parted from him again.

CHAPTER THIRTY

Over the next several days after that Thursday night, Max's happiness was restored. He reminded himself from time to time that all would be well if he could just remember never again to bring up the idea of getting a divorce. But he went further—he made certain that everything he said or did betrayed no discontent of any kind with the status quo. Such guardedness added still more tension to his daily life, but he found it a small price to pay to keep Paul from experiencing anxiety about the security of Max's family. He even consciously avoided any reference to the kids now, as well as to Michelle. In Max's view, he'd damaged their relationship by suggesting a divorce. If there was any estrangement between them now, it was his own fault, and he'd have to work at getting things back to normal.

Paul seemed content enough, generally, but he was often remote, as though he might be worrying about something he didn't want to talk about. Max consoled himself by thinking that Paul was probably worried about whether his grandmother would be okay on their trip to Spain. They were supposed to leave on the following Monday. Paul was going down to Savannah to pick her up over the weekend, and once he left for Savannah, Max wouldn't see him again until he came back from Spain. Two whole weeks. Even then, he probably wouldn't see him until he'd taken his grandmother back home to Savannah and returned to Atlanta—and how long would that be? Probably at least three weeks altogether. He dreaded the separation, but he kept it to himself, wary of being perceived as complaining, determined to accept the fact that family members came first —Paul's as well as his own.

Max wasn't the only one to notice a change in Paul.

Michelle thought he was behaving a little strangely. He turned more responsibilities over to her at the office, and sometimes she passed the glass door of his office and saw him just sitting there, staring out the window. On Thursday, Michelle decided to ask him if anything was wrong. She opened the door and leaned through the doorway without coming in.

"Paul, is everything all right with you?"

He was doodling on a notepad; he looked up at her, surprised. "Sure. Why?"

"You seem so not here—almost like Jake." She smiled.

He smiled back. "Just thinking about Nana—and the trip. Did I tell you how she found her great-niece?" When Michelle shook her head, he said, "She wrote a letter to her sister—even though she knew her sister had been dead for years."

"What?"

"Yes, really. Almost as though she knew the letter would be forwarded to her sister's daughter—who then sent it to *her* daughter, Nana's great-niece, in Barcelona."

"Wow, that's a clever lady."

"No, not really. I would say it was just luck—except that I think God's always been on Nana's side."

Michelle laughed. Then she came all the way through the door into the office. "Let me get that out of your way." She reached for the picture of Roxie, which was still propped against the portfolio on the floor.

"No, no, leave it here, if you don't mind. You can get it next week when I'm gone. I've been meaning to ask you—did Jake tell you when he did that?"

"Yes. He did it at Highland just before he came home for the summer. He said it was from a memory of a day on the houseboat. Roxie was just climbing back on board from swimming in the lake."

"Hm. Does Roxie wear a life jacket when she goes swimming?"

"Roxie in a life jacket? Good Lord, no. Swims like a fish. She would have you know that she's the only student at St. Joseph's Academy to have certification in life-saving. And to tell you the truth—I wouldn't tell her—if I were drowning, I'd want Roxanne Maxwell on lifeguard duty."

* * *

Paul was not unaware of his distraction, only that others noticed it. He'd gone through the past week not so much like one who's anticipating his own departure as like one who is awaiting an arrival—of someone, or a letter or package, not knowing the day or time of the arrival. When he'd met Max at Gino's yesterday afternoon, there was a tension. It seemed to Paul that Max was not behaving as ingenuously as he used to, he was not his spontaneous self; the whole atmosphere had been strained—the more so because both of them were acting as if everything were normal. And then, as he lay in bed last night, Paul realized: *He knows. He knows it's coming to an end.* It made him raise his head and shoulders from the bed, and he lay there, resting on his elbows. *Is it coming to an end?* Max seemed far away, across an ocean, already a memory.

And that Thursday night, he returned to St. Andrew's, a place he never would have thought he'd see again. But there he was, walking down the dark hallway again, toward the room at the end where light and talk and laughter came from. He'd waited until he knew the meeting was over, when there would be a few stragglers having coffee.

That afternoon, on a sudden impulse, he'd called Father Bazenski: "Tell me, Father, what is wrong with love?"

"Absolutely nothing."

"Ever?"

"Ever." There was a pause then and a silence. Father Bazenski said, "Come back, Paul. But this time, bring your life jacket."

And here he was. They turned and greeted him, still seated on the worn-out sofa and chairs around a coffee table. If they were surprised to see him, they didn't let it show. Malcolm, the doctor, moved over on the sofa to make room for him. There was someone new there, a kid, younger than Johnny the musician, maybe eighteen or nineteen. He was small, with thick light brown hair and very blue eyes. He said he was Jesse.

"I've been on vacation up north, so I didn't see you when you came last week," he said, evidently feeling, in a child-like way, that he should explain his unknown-ness to Paul.

"Nice to meet you," said Paul, politely.

"We were just talking about you," answered the boy.

Paul blushed and frowned, but he looked at the faces of the others. They wore gentle, almost affectionate, smiles that said, "Don't be afraid. You are not strange here."

But then Jesse said, "Yes. We were talking about love." And Paul knew they'd been discussing not him so much as what he'd said last week, perhaps his denial of personal choice. He hoped that was true—he wouldn't have to do any apologetic explaining.

"We'll come back to that." Father Bazenski said. And then they talked. They talked about everything—the Braves, a new movie, and it turned out that Steve had auditioned for a part. They talked about Jesse's parents in upstate New York, and how they were encouraging him toward a possible vocation in the priesthood. Father Bernie said he shouldn't be in a hurry; if the call was there, it would still be there in a year or two. Malcolm told them about an incident with a patient who had recognized him from a party he'd attended more than three years ago—and would past associations never end? The consensus was no, they wouldn't end, so they must be accepted, lived with somehow. Paul began to feel that this odd mix of men were his best friends, the friends he'd never had, friends who were neither objects of desire, nor the "other" kind—those with whom one is never completely oneself.

He went over to the counter and poured a cup of coffee, feeling more at home in the shabby little room than he'd ever felt anywhere in his life—not just accepted, but *known* and accepted, as he was. It was peculiar and ironic—to feel so "known" among men who didn't even know his last name. He realized that he was beginning to *trust* them, and at the same time, he knew he'd never really trusted men before— *any* men, gay or straight.

"Okay," said Father Bazenski. "Let's talk about love." The chatter slowly died down and stopped.

Johnny spoke up. "Well, you all know about Bill and me. I want to tell you, by the way, he's doing fine. Got a gig with a group out in California." He glanced at Paul and added, "Bill and I were lovers. Bill is how I discovered some things about myself." Paul looked puzzled, and Johnny said, "Bill's a predator. He doesn't know it, though."

Father Bazenski interjected, "Only because he doesn't know he has an entirely different problem. He thinks his predatory behavior is due to being gay."

Paul wanted to ask for more details about this Bill—he'd known a lot of gay men who were predators. But then he remembered—the behavior was what Bill *did*, it wasn't what he *was*. There was no bitterness in Johnny's remark, and Paul understood why. Johnny wasn't blaming his former lover—because he understood that this Bill, in blaming his behavior on something he thought he was, made him a victim much more than those he victimized. He looked at the spike-haired kid and thought he was more grown-up than most grown-ups he knew.

Jesse said, "Oh, yeah. Predators." He looked thoughtful for a moment. "A parable, maybe. You know, there are some things you can't talk about—can't explain—in any other way."

And Paul made his first contribution to the discussion: "Yes. Like art. Art exists because there are some things that can't be said in any other way. And parable is an art form."

Jesse smiled at him in agreement. "Okay, let's try a parable, a parable about a predator." To Paul's surprise, the others leaned a little toward the pale young man, who sat with both hands clasped together between his blue-jeaned knees, scrunched down like a small boy in the big, faded brown and blue tweed chair.

"There's a group of lambs, maybe three or four, playing together on green grass. Every so often, they eat a little of the grass, but they're just playing, enjoying being alive, you know? They're just enjoying being. They have a shepherd. And they're loved—so much and so well, they don't even know they're loved—because they never have to think about it. Like the grass—it's always there. They don't have to go hunting for it. Being loved and taken care of, for them, is— just life. They don't want anything because they have everything.

"Now, there's a lion nearby. He's watching. He's wanting. He's wanting because he *doesn't* have. He doesn't have what they have, and he craves it with an irresistible craving. "

"It's hunger," Paul said, "just hunger."

"Stronger than that," said Jesse.

"Let's call it what it is—*desire*," said Father Bernie. "That's stronger than hunger."

"Yes, but let's understand that desire," interjected Father Bazenski, "its power, or strength. You said it's 'irresistible,' so it's very powerful. It can never be fulfilled—like a gaping void—a wound. And without knowing it's there, the lion spends his whole life trying to fill it, trying to heal that wound. Why do you suppose he does that? Why do you suppose he can't just let it go, forget about it?"

Everyone was silent for a moment. "Because," said Jesse quietly, "it's the way we are—the way we *all* are. 'De-sire' *means* 'of the father.' The lambs don't have that desire only because they don't have that aching void."

"But," said Paul, a little strongly, so that it surprised him, "it's just hunger." And then he added, "*It's not love.*"

"Actually," said Jesse, "that's exactly what it is—love. You just don't know that's what it is if you don't have it—you *can't* know. You have no experience of it, no memory of it."

Everyone was quiet, listening to Jesse's parable, and maybe to their own thoughts as well. Paul was quiet, too. It was *his* story. It may have been everyone's story, and not just those in the room—but everyone's. Suddenly, he could feel the blood draining from his face as he saw—*from the inside* — a boy, a small child, alone and frightened in the dark— abandoned. He could feel the child's fear and helplessness. Then he forced himself outside the child in order to look at the child's face, expecting to see his own, but instead, it was his father's face he saw....

It was Malcolm who broke the silence. "Maybe there's never been any kind of story *except* a love story," he said.

Father Bernie added, "Sometimes I think the only reason we're here is to learn how to love."

"The lion didn't know how because he had no experience of it," observed Johnny. "Neither did Bill."

"But wait a minute. You know what? The lambs don't either," said Malcolm suddenly. And Paul remembered thinking that Roxie and Jake didn't know how blessed they were. "No," Malcolm continued thoughtfully, with a rueful smile. "They do know—that's why *they* don't have to learn ...but the rest of us do."

They were quiet for a long moment then, until Father Bazenski stood up and stretched, and the others did, too. It was after 10:00.

Paul didn't want to go home, to bed, to sleep. He went back to the gallery.

CHAPTER THIRTY-ONE

"When you meet the Buddha, what should you do?"
"Kill him."
"Why?"
"So that you may become him."
It was a dialogue Paul remembered from a Humanities course in college. He hadn't understood it. The professor, a Buddhist, told him he couldn't understand it because he wasn't a Buddhist. Paul realized it was the point of view of Jesse's lion. The lion had been deprived. And none of us can 'know' things except by our *experience* of them.

He sat at his desk, his chair swiveled around to look out the window. He couldn't see the night sky from that window because the building was not tall enough. Instead, he saw only the buildings opposite the window. He didn't feel his removal from the fray of a living city as he did from the balcony of his apartment. Here, he was in the middle of it, where vision was limited.

He took the elevator down to the mezzanine, turned on the lights on the far wall, where "The Lion's Heart" was hanging, so big it looked as though it were the wall itself. He didn't stay long, only a minute or two; he was remembering John Mayfield, remembering Max, and finally, Jake. He thought, *I didn't show this painting to Jake; it was Jake who showed it to me.* "The Lion's Heart" was glory and emptiness—passion imploded on itself, barren self-love. It was glory—but it was a glorification of emptiness, of a void. He turned off the lights and went back up to his office.

He sat there leaning back in his chair, looking at Jake's drawing of Roxie, where it was still on the floor, propped against the wall. Her face, thrown back a little in laughter, was made of little bits of light, like countless drops of sunlight glinting off water. He'd never seen anything like it, but it wasn't Jake's technique he saw, no matter how new or different it was. What marked it was the same thing that marked authenticity whenever he saw it—vision.

He lost himself in that vision now. *Roxie.* In that moment, Paul loved her, and he discovered in that same moment that he knew *how* to love her. Outside *yourself,* he thought, outside your own needs, your own desires. Was that what Nana meant when she said there's no love without sacrifice? Every little girl is a Roxie, he thought, a Roxie who can make sunlight laugh—if you know how to see her as her brother had done. And now, Paul did, too. Art was, after all, not the vision *of* love—but *by* love. Love overcomes self in order to see, in order to love—that's how it's done, that's *how* the wound is...healed.

And in loving Roxie in that moment, he loved every little girl in the world—known and unknown. And each one, along with all their brothers, was unspeakably precious to him. The fecundity of that love overwhelmed him. It was the Russian doll, endlessly begetting itself. *Only get outside yourself— outside your pain, the prison of your desire, the prison of your selfness.*

Paul got up from his chair and went to the janitor's closet where, months ago, he'd seen the Mexican cleaning woman at her prayers. The door to the closet was locked. He slumped against the wall opposite the locked door and slid to the floor. He was too late—and the door was locked. Somewhere in there was a gaudy, glitter-covered candle, hidden from him in darkness. Facing the locked door, he found himself praying, whispering aloud, "Help me. Help me to remove my own self. I can't do it on my own."

Eventually, he got up, stumbled back to his office and sat down at his desk. He was completely empty of all thought or feeling. As he started to set his computer in sleep mode, he saw that he had an email from the gallery in Barcelona. They were asking him to re-consider the job offer. It was still open. Would he accept if they offered a higher salary?

Paul covered his face with his hands, laughing softly. *Oh, you are too obvious, You are just too obvious.* He wanted to laugh out loud at the mundaneness of it, the down-to-earth ordinariness of it, but he was exhausted. He glanced at the clock on his desk: almost 1:00 in the morning. But he had work to do. First, he'd answer the email—and then he had some letters to write, three letters, in fact. He'd leave a letter to Michelle on her desk, telling her about his decision and expressing his belief that she'd be a very good director of the Hunter Gallery; he'd write the chairman of the board of directors, expressing his gratitude for the board's confidence in him, and apologizing for the abruptness of his resignation —and he'd recommend Michelle as his replacement. He'd mail that letter in the post...and he'd mail a letter to Max at his office address. It would take him quite a while, but he'd finish long before the gallery opened in the morning, and then he'd go home to pack, and to call Nana—and maybe Father Thomas, too. And—oh, yes—he reminded himself: he had to cancel the return flight from Spain.

* * *

Five days later, at lunchtime on Wednesday, Max was at the car dealership with Jake.

This was *not* how he'd imagined it. He tried to be excited —he told himself he should be excited for Jake's sake—but everything he said turned to ashes in his mouth. Like everything he said all the time, no matter where he was or what the situation was—everything he said felt false, felt like a lie.

"Your mother doesn't need to know—not until we get the title and finish the paperwork. And then she won't be able to do anything about it."

"I don't know, Dad," Jake stood there with his hands in

the back pockets of his jeans, clearly feeling awkward. "This thing cost a *lot* of money. Are you sure? Maybe you guys could do something else now—get a car later—for Christmas, maybe, or graduation."

He didn't say it out loud, but Max knew what he was thinking: "later" meant when Mom wouldn't be lied to, when maybe she'd be in agreement. Max had made a big show of having the car driven round to where they were standing with the salesman. Jake was uncomfortable and Max knew it. It made him angry. What kind of ungrateful kid wouldn't want a sports car for his birthday?

"Well, look," he said. "Take it out and see what you think...."

"But I don't have my license yet."

The salesman, sensing the danger of a lost sale, said, "You could take him, Mr. Maxwell. He's got his temporary license. We don't usually let somebody with a temporary license do a test drive, but if you went with him...."

"I don't have time now." He felt like slapping Jake. His lack of enthusiasm had ruined what little hope Max had of ever smiling again.

"I'll take him," said the salesman.

"Whatever," said Max bitterly. "I've got to get back to the office." He turned to go and said to the salesman over his shoulder. "When you're done, you can either take him home or put him in a cab."

* * *

For years afterward, Michelle remembered that moment —five after three. It was raining that day. She had what she called a summer cold and stayed home. John Barfield, the board chair, had told her that she was under consideration to be the new director of the gallery, since Paul's sudden resignation last week. She would never understand his mysterious departure—she came to work on Friday morning and found a letter he'd left on her desk. She was still sitting there, too stunned to think, when the phone rang; it was John, saying that he'd had an email from Paul giving him the news. Paul had told him in the email that a formal letter of resignation would come later in the post. And before he rang off, he said the board would consider her as the new director. It was clear that John strongly disapproved of Paul's leaving so suddenly, regardless of the job offer at the Barcelona gallery, which, in his view, didn't amount to much.

Michelle tried to agree with John, but actually, she was too hurt to think about any sort of professional ethic in Paul's sudden resignation and departure. He had become very dear to her, a close personal friend. She couldn't believe he left the way he did just because of a job offer in Spain. That wasn't Paul. It remained a mystery for her. In any case, if she was being considered for director, it was no time to miss work and stay in bed, so she'd brought work home with her. She could do nearly everything with the laptop and the phone—at least for a day or two.

She was in the little room that she used as a home office, just off the kitchen, sitting in front of the computer screen. She was wearing shorts and a tee-shirt, she remembered, the gray shorts and white tee-shirt that she later threw away. They were never worn again.

She was barefoot. Her hair was pulled up and clasped together at the back of her head with a clamp, and even though she was foggy from an antihistamine, she was sipping a glass of wine as she worked on a spreadsheet for inventory ...when she heard the front door chime. Somehow she knew as soon as she heard the chime. She stood up and watched Gladys leave the kitchen to answer the door. And she was still standing there when Gladys returned. Gladys stayed outside the doorway of the little office, like she didn't want to come in. Her eyes were round and her mouth was in a tight, straight line.

She said, "Somebody at the door, Mrs. Maxwell. Wants to speak with you." Her voice squeaked.

"Well, who is it?" asked Michelle.

"State Police."

"And what do they want?"

"Wouldn't tell me, ma'am. Asked for you."

* * *

Max sat at the table at Gino's, where he and Paul always sat on Wednesday afternoons at four. He took the letter out of his wallet and read it again:

My Dear Max,

Nana and I are leaving for Barcelona, but by the time you receive this at your office, you will already know that. I have a job waiting for me there, not as good as the job I had at Hunter, but a good one, and it will give me an opportunity to learn a lot. Nana's great-niece has invited us to stay with her until we can find a place of our own. Looking back, I think this—maybe all of this—became inevitable months ago, when you told me to ask her what she wanted.

What I feel now, and what I think—about us, I mean. I love you. No less now than I ever did. That's why I have to do this like a coward, in a letter, because I know I would never be able to do it in person.

My gay friends are right about one thing: Love is never wrong. But the trouble with that rather righteous-sounding moralism is that whether to love was never the question. How to love is what's so damned hard. How doesn't affect just us—but everybody, everywhere and always. Otherwise, it's just us loving ourselves in each other.

I never knew anything about that because I never loved until you. I'm trying to learn now, but I'm just a beginner, trying to get the basics. All I know so far is—one, it's what we choose to do that makes us what we are—not the other way around. And two, there's no love without sacrifice.

We've both been wounded. Loving you healed me. I'll

always be scarred, always have to struggle—but I don't think you will, not after you recover from the pain I'm causing you now. You are surrounded by people who already know how to love you. And that will be your healing.

Forgive me.

Paul

Max re-folded the letter very small and put it back in his wallet. He said he was gone—*but it's Wednesday, it's 4:00....*
And so Max was sitting in the leather armchair, looking out at the rain through the window at Gino's. Michelle hadn't stopped trying to phone him for the past hour, but he couldn't talk to her, not right now. He turned from the window to look down into the glass of bourbon over ice, untouched on the little laminated table at his elbow. His fingers moved the glass slightly—not much, just enough to make a small light from somewhere glitter across a piece of ice. And in that moment, he knew. All hope was dead.

How strange it was—all the trembling fear, the dread, ended in a fraction of a second, in a passing glint off the surface of a piece of ice. He knew Paul wasn't coming—not today, not ever. He would never see him again. He knew with an irrevocable certainty that dipped down inside him like a scimitar, in one sweeping, sudden thrust of pain, so deep it paralyzed him. He couldn't breathe, his heart stopped beating. He wanted desperately to get up, to shove aside the little laminated table, even knock the glass over— what did it matter? Nothing mattered. He wanted to leave, get a cab to the airport, and get the next flight out to Barcelona, to find him—to make it not so. Scenes from old black and white movies flickered in his mind like adolescent fantasies, lovers falling into each other's arms in the rain as some kind of symphonic music played in the background. The stuff of movies, of imagination. Drowning in joyful embrace...drowning.

He looked back at the rain. Was it because he'd wanted to leave Michelle and the kids—*and said so*? His fault—he should have kept that to himself, at least for a while, until Paul could see, as he did, that it was the only answer. But Paul could not accept the moral responsibility—or *wouldn't* accept it, maybe. Was that it? Yes. No. More...other. It didn't matter. There would a lifetime, an empty lifetime, to ask why.

The rain was coming down in heavy gray sheets now. Taxis drove past the window, throwing water over the curb to the sidewalk, where pedestrians jumped aside under their umbrellas. His cell phone vibrated in his pocket again. He knew it was Michelle. Finally, he breathed, and took a deep draught of the bourbon. Then he reached into his jacket and got out his wallet again, dropped a twenty on the table, and went out into the rain.

ABOUT THE AUTHOR

Dena Hunt taught English at the University of New Orleans until her conversion to Christianity in 1984. Following her reception into the Roman Catholic Church, she returned to her native Georgia and taught in rural high schools until she retired. She did not start writing until after her retirement. Currently, she has several short stories in print and online, as well as reviews and essays. *The Lion's Heart* is her second novel. The first, *Treason*, was published by Sophia Institute Press in the spring of 2013 and won the Gold Medal in Religious Fiction in the 2014 IPPY Awards.

For a complete list of FQP books, please visit our website: www.fullquiverpublishing.com or email us at fullquiverpublishing@gmail.com

FQ Publishing
PO Box 244
Pakenham, ON K0A2X0
Canada

www.fullquiverpublishing.com
www.thelionsheart.ca

Book clubs: Contact the publisher for bulk rates and discussion questions: fullquiverpublishing@gmail.com